Whiskers and Warrants –
A Norwegian Forest Cat Café
Cozy Mystery –
Book 3

by

Jinty James

Whiskers and Warrants - A
Norwegian Forest Cat Café Cozy
Mystery – Book 3

by

Jinty James

ISBN: 9781075850226

DEDICATION

For Annie, my beautiful Norwegian Forest Cat.

And to all my wonderful readers. Thank you.

CHAPTER 1

"I thought we would be the only students," Zoe whispered to Lauren. Her brunette pixie cut seemed to flop a little in disappointment.

They were at a fancy café in Sacramento on a Monday night. The gleam of the maple hardwood floors reflected off the white painted walls. Downlights provided plenty of illumination and an extended counter on one side of the room sported a huge espresso machine. On the other side of the room, white wooden tables with maple colored chairs completed the look.

"So did I," Lauren murmured.

Attending the advanced latte art class seemed such a good idea at the time – but now she was wondering if they'd just wasted two hundred dollars.

The masterclass had been billed as learning from an international barista champion, only two students per session, yet there were three other students in the room.

"This is so exciting!" A plump woman in her late thirties with caramel-brown hair beamed at them. Standing beside her was a slim teen around sixteen, staring at her phone. "Isn't it, Casey?" She nudged the girl.

"I guess." The brunette teenager looked up from her phone, shrugged, then swiped at the screen.

"I thought this would be the perfect way to do some mother-daughter bonding," the woman confided to Lauren and Zoe. "I hardly see Casey right now – she's busy working part-time at a coffee shop as well as going to high school – but when she told me she wanted to attend this class, I thought, why shouldn't I come too?"

"Are you a barista?" Lauren asked.

"Me? No, no." The woman laughed. "Although–" she leaned toward them "—we have just bought our first espresso machine." She glanced fondly at her daughter. "Casey told us not long after she started training as a barista that we needed to get an espresso machine if we wanted to drink decent coffee."

"I thought this class was for experienced baristas." Zoe sent Lauren a puzzled glance.

"It is." The woman kept her voice low. "But I thought they probably wouldn't mind if I tagged along with Casey. She's tried to show me how to make a heart and a tulip, but there are so many things I need to remember." She laughed. "Don't hold the jug like this, Mom. You're doing it wrong. Put the nose in closer."

"It does take a while," Lauren told her encouragingly. "I couldn't do a heart my first time – or my fifth."

"And now Lauren's hearts are the best," Zoe boasted. "Along with her tulips and rosettas – and her cats!"

"Cats?" The mother looked curious. "How do you make a cat?"

"By drawing on the features." A short man in his fifties entered the conversation. He wore spectacles and his dark thinning hair revealed a large bald patch. "You can either make a shape like a heart – or a dot, I believe it's called – and then draw on the eyes and whiskers using a digital thermometer dipped into the crema surrounding the shape. Another way – although I call it the cheat's way – is to spoon the foam onto the crema and then draw on the features."

"My goodness," the woman said admiringly. "I had no idea."

"I'm Frank," the man said, nodding at them.

"I'm Lauren, and this is my cousin Zoe."

"We run the Norwegian Forest Cat Café in Gold Leaf Valley," Zoe added.

"That's over an hour from here, isn't it?" the woman asked.

"Yes." Lauren nodded.

"Did you say a cat café?" Her eyes widened.

"Yep." Zoe grinned. "Lauren's cat, Annie, shows customers to their table."

"Oh, my. That sounds wonderful. You two are dedicated, coming to Sacramento for this class. Oh – I'm Judy, and you've already met my daughter." She looked at the girl fondly.

Casey glanced up from her phone. "I thought there were only two students per class." She frowned.

"I thought so, too," Zoe replied.

"Maybe they'll increase the number of teachers," Frank said. "Although Giovanni Voltozini is supposed to be teaching this class. That's why I came."

"Buon giorno, everybody." A tall, dark-haired man swept into the room, carrying a tablet. He looked to be in his early forties, with handsome expressive features and a seven p.m. shadow. "This is the advanced latte art class. And I am Giovanni Voltozini. Welcome!"

He paused, as if waiting for a smattering of applause. When none came, he continued undaunted, "Tonight, we will attempt many things. Swans, peacocks, and perhaps a bleeding heart – if we have time. You will be working very hard. By the finish of class tonight, you should all be able to achieve an excellent swan or peacock. Some of you—" his assessing gaze swept over all five of them "—should be able to do much, much more than that. Because you are all experienced baristas, no?"

Judy cleared her throat and looked embarrassed. "Um – no."

"I'm not either," Frank admitted.

"Then why did you sign up for the class?" The Italian's dark eyes flashed with annoyance.

"Mom thought it would be good for us to do something together," the teen piped up when everyone else was silent.

"And you - you have experience?"

"Yes." It sounded like *"Duh."*

"She's the best barista at the café," Judy said. "Maybe you know it? It's five blocks from here and it's called The Roasted Hipster. And she only started there a few months ago."

"Good." Giovanni sounded relieved. "And you two?" He scrutinized Lauren and Zoe.

"We run a café in Gold Leaf Valley," Lauren said, feeling a little intimidated. At home, she was confident with her skills. But now, in this setting, with an Italian international barista champion staring at her, she wondered if all her know-how would desert her when she needed it.

"Lauren is awesome with her latte art," Zoe told him.

"And you?" He gave her a piercing glance.

Zoe squirmed. "I can do a heart, and a tulip, and a rosetta – I think I'm better at rosettas – all that wiggling. Lauren taught me everything."

"We shall see just how good you really are," the Italian proclaimed, still giving Zoe an assessing look. "And you, sir? You said you are not experienced?" He glanced at Frank.

"No, but I've read up on it," Frank replied eagerly. "And watched online videos. I've tried at home but I can only get a faint outline. Coffee is going to be my new thing. I've retired early and need something to do. I'm going to start a coffee blog and monetize it."

"Awesome," Casey the teenager murmured, sounding impressed. "Maybe I should do that."

"Reading and watching is not the same thing at all." Giovanni waved his hand dismissively. "You two—" he glowered at Judy and Frank "—have much to learn. Tcha! I shall have to bring in someone to help you. Luckily," he paused, with the air of expecting them to realize just how lucky they were, "my partner is still here. She will help the beginners. The others will learn with *me!*"

"About that." Zoe raised a hand. "We thought there would be only two students per class."

"Yes." Judy nodded. "That's right."

"You all have a chance to learn from *me*." Giovanni placed his hand on his heart. "I have won many barista titles, and people clamor to work with me all the time. All the time! And now, with my partner Amy helping, it is practically the same as two students per class. It is better this way. The beginners will not slow down the advanced." He cast his gaze over Lauren, Zoe, and Casey.

A slender redhead in her thirties entered the room, and stopped when she caught sight of everyone.

"Oh, you've already started. I'm sorry, Gio, there was a glitch with the bookings. There are five people instead of two."

"It is no matter," the Italian said grandly. "You will help the beginners, Amy." He pointed to Judy and Frank. "You will be at that end of the machine." He motioned toward the large, gleaming silver espresso machine. It dwarfed the one Lauren and Zoe used in their café. "My advanced students will learn from me at the other end."

"Oh, but—" Amy's protest fell silent as the Italian frowned at her. "Very well." She sighed.

"I wonder what that was all about," Zoe whispered out of the side of her mouth to Lauren.

"There will be no talking unless you need to ask a question." Giovanni's gaze zeroed in on Zoe. "We shall be busy – very, very busy. And afterwards, if any of you have reached a satisfactory standard, you will receive a certificate."

"Ooh, I'd love a certificate." Judy looked excited. "I'll be able to show everyone at tennis club."

"Mom," Casey groaned in embarrassment.

Giovanni clapped his hands. "Come! It is time to learn." He looked at his tablet. "But first, I must take this roll call. Lauren Crenshaw."

Lauren raised her hand.

"Zoe Crenshaw."

Zoe raised her hand.

After the Italian had checked off the remaining three people, he clapped his hands once more. "Lauren, Zoe, and Casey, you are with me." He swept towards the silver espresso machine.

Lauren, Zoe and the teen followed him.

"Judy and Frank," Amy called out. "We will work at this end of the machine." She smiled to them as she beckoned them toward her.

"We shall do split double shots," Giovanni informed them. He filled the portafilter with freshly ground beans, pressed them down with an impressive looking black and gold metal tamper, inserted the portafilter into the grouphead, and put two round shallow cups underneath. He repeated the actions until there were four cups waiting to be filled with espresso.

"Have any of you worked with such a magnificent machine?" He patted the shining beast. "It can make many espressos at once."

"Which is good, since there are three of us at this end," Zoe muttered to Lauren.

"I will show you this only once, and then you can take turns extracting the coffee and steaming the milk," he informed them.

"What will you do?" Casey asked.

"I shall supervise! I will instruct each of you personally as to your designs. And tell you where you go wrong." His gaze lingered on Zoe.

"Is it my imagination or doesn't he like me?" Zoe murmured to Lauren.

"No talking!" Giovanni scolded her.

"Sorry," Zoe muttered, her cheeks turning pink.

Her cousin was a livewire, but Lauren hoped that Zoe could enjoy tonight, while not drawing the ire of the teacher.

"Your milk must be thick and glossy, like wet paint," Giovanni informed them as he steamed the milk in a jug. The hissing noise of the milk wand soothed Lauren.

"See?" He banged the stainless-steel jug on the counter twice and swirled it, pointing to the contents. White, shiny milk without any bubbles filled the jug.

"Cool," Casey murmured.

The Italian gave her an approving glance.

"Now, you each have a cup." He placed a round white cup in front of them, filled with a single shot of espresso with honey-colored crema.

The long wooden counter gave each of them enough room to stand and work on their designs.

Lauren peeked at the other end of the bench. Amy was filling the portafilter and speaking to Judy and Frank in low tones.

"First, I want to see if you tell me the truth and you are experienced," Giovanni said. "Make me a rosetta." He finished steaming milk in two more pitchers and placed them in front of the trio.

Lauren focused on mixing some of the milk into the espresso. Then she changed the angle of the jug, pointing the nose at the center of her cup and concentrated on wiggling backward. She finished with lifting the pitcher up and pulling it through the decorative pattern. A leaf bloomed on the surface of the coffee.

"Bellissimo!" The Italian peered over her shoulder. "Perfect! You should have no trouble with what you will learn tonight."

Lauren smiled, pleased with his praise.

She watched her cousin pulling through her design.

"Too fast!" Giovanni scolded Zoe. "Look, you have slopped over the edge." He pointed to the brown liquid staining the side of the cup. "You have ruined the pattern."

Lauren glanced at Zoe's design. It had less definition than the ones she normally made at their café.

"He made me nervous," Zoe whispered to her. "I was trying to be so careful and then realized I filled up the cup too much, so I rushed on the pull through before I overflowed." She gazed at her work in dismay.

"It's okay," Lauren whispered back. "I know you can do it."

"Yes," Giovanni boomed as he looked at the teen's effort. "Good. But you must not take short cuts. You must practice, practice, practice. And when you become a premier barista, then you can work anywhere – and name your price."

"Really?" Casey looked at him, impressed.

"Only if you have what it takes. By the end of class tonight I will know if you are cut out to be a top barista, like me." Pride shone in his eyes.

"Cool."

"He didn't say that to me," Zoe muttered to her cousin. She sounded discouraged.

"I know you'll prove him wrong," Lauren told her. She hoped her cousin would. "Just pretend you're at our café."

"I'll try," Zoe whispered, looking a little more cheerful.

The sound of a woman giggling cut through the sudden silence. Lauren saw Judy, Casey's mom, pointing at a cappuccino cup and laughing. Amy, Judy's teacher, smiled at her student.

"You must not be distracted," Giovanni scolded Lauren. "We do not care what they are doing over there. We will now attempt a swan."

"Awesome!" Casey's eyes widened, some of her "teen cool" attitude disappearing.

"You." He pointed to Zoe. "Must watch and learn. No talking. Since you are in the advanced class, I expect you to have advanced skills. Otherwise, you can join the *beginners*." He said the last word with a slight sneer in his voice.

Lauren was just about to open her mouth to defend Zoe when her cousin shook her head.

"Now, watch."

Giovanni extracted a split espresso shot, foamed the milk, and then began to pour the milk into the cappuccino cup, his movements economical and precise.

"Wow," Casey murmured as a swan took shape on the surface of the coffee.

"Now you will all try." Giovanni watched them like a hawk as they made their own espresso shots and steamed the milk.

Lauren held her breath as she began to pour the micro foam into her cup. Should she and Zoe stay until the end of the class? Or should they walk out? She didn't care for the barista's attitude – or the way he'd spoken to Zoe – or herself.

She made a rosetta for the base of the swan, then worked on the wings, neck, and finally a little heart for the head. Was it good enough?

Finished, she peered over at her cousin. Zoe bit her lip as she poured the glossy milk into her cup, her movements careful.

"Yes!" Zoe jumped on the spot. "I did it!"

"Let me see." Giovanni studied her effort. "Hmm. You need more definition on this wing, and more ripples down here." He pointed to underneath the wing. "But you will be staying in this group for now."

Relief flickered over Zoe's face.

Giovanni scrutinized Lauren's swan. "Yes, you have a good grasp of the art," he praised her. "But you need just a touch more definition on the neck."

"Done!" Casey waved a hand.

Giovanni strode to the teen.

"It is sloppy." He frowned at her. "You are young, yes, but you must pay attention when I demonstrate to you. Otherwise you will not become a great barista." He sighed. "I will show you again." He turned to Lauren and Zoe.

"You two will make another swan, and call me when you're finished."

Lauren and Zoe worked quietly while Giovanni showed Casey the precise movements involved in creating a swan.

"We did it!" Zoe waved a hand in the air to attract their teacher's attention.

"Let me see." Giovanni strode over in two quick steps and peered first at Lauren's attempt, and then at Zoe's. "Better, both of you. Make two more each and show me."

"High five!" Zoe held up her palm to Lauren.

They quietly slapped hands, then Zoe took over making the new espressos.

After another two swans, Giovanni proclaimed himself pleased with their progress.

"And now," he told them, "We shall progress to peacocks. You too, Casey."

"Cool!" Casey grinned.

"We shall start off with a rosetta base and continue from there." He clapped his hands. "Let's get to work!"

"No." Giovanni sounded exasperated as he spoke to Zoe a few minutes later. "Not like that." He grabbed the milk jug and a new cup filled with espresso and showed her in swift motions exactly how to create a peacock.

"Wow," Zoe murmured, her eyes wide, when he showed her the finished design, the creature's tail fanned out across the width of the cup.

"You must practice, practice, practice," he told the three of them. "Now all of you make another peacock."

The milk wand hissed as Lauren, Zoe, and Casey steamed their milk, then set to work.

"Better," Giovanni said grudgingly as they each showed him their latest attempt.

Judy's giggle drifted over from the other end of the counter. Lauren glanced over at the beginner's group. Frank and Judy looked like they were enjoying themselves. Judy pointed to her cup, while Frank peered over her shoulder, a grin on his face.

Giovanni clapped his hands. Lauren swung back to face him.

"Sorry," she murmured.

"Beginners can laugh and enjoy themselves because they do not know any better," he told her. "But you are the advanced class." He waved his hand, indicating all three of them. "You are here to work, and improve your skills. Now, make another peacock."

Lauren heard Casey groan under her breath.

"Gio," Amy's clear voice sounded. "Class is finished for the night. We've run over by ten minutes."

Lauren watched what looked like relief flicker over Giovanni's face. Had they been that bad at advanced latte art?

"All right." He nodded. "I expect you to practice at home." He turned to Lauren, Zoe, and Casey. "Every day."

"I thought we could have a make-up class next week," Amy's voice carried over to them. "To say sorry for the glitch tonight. I can teach the advanced class next week, and Gio, you can spend time with Judy and Frank."

"That would be great." Frank turned around and beamed at Giovanni. "I can't wait to work with you."

Giovanni frowned and opened his mouth to speak.

Amy gave him what Lauren could only describe as a school- marm look and Giovanni closed his mouth.

"If the calendar is clear for next week," Giovanni said grudgingly.

"It is," Amy assured him. "Thanks for coming tonight, everyone. We'll see you back here next Monday at the same time."

The five students filed out of the room.

"That was very informative," Frank remarked. "I made a heart and Amy said I was on the way to making a tulip. I can't wait until next week. What did you three make?" He studied Lauren, Zoe, and Casey.

"A swan," Zoe replied.

"And then we moved on to peacocks," Casey added.

"Peacocks?" Judy placed a hand over her heart. "That's wonderful, honey. How on earth do you make a peacock out of milk? You'll have to show me when we get home."

"Oh-kay," Casey replied in a long-suffering tone.

"It was nice meeting you," Lauren told them.

"I guess we'll see you next week." Zoe grinned at them. "We're parked right outside. How about you?"

"Us too," Judy assured them.

"Yep." Frank nodded.

They left the café. The summer evening sun was just sinking toward the horizon. Lauren and Zoe got into their car while Judy and Casey entered a beige station wagon. Frank walked a few yards down the street and opened the door of a black compact car.

"I can do a swan!" Zoe fastened her seatbelt. "It might have been a little wonky – like my peacock – but it was definitely a swan – and a peacock."

"Now we have to practice." Lauren turned on the ignition.

"Yeah." Zoe sounded a little downhearted. "Giovanni seems to be big on that."

"I know." Lauren pulled out onto the road, passing Judy, and Frank.

Zoe waved to them out of her window.

"But I'm glad we came tonight, aren't you?" Lauren asked her cousin.

"Yep. But I wonder what that was about with Giovanni and Amy?"

"You mean the booking glitch?" Lauren asked as she stared straight ahead at the road.

"Uh-huh. And how he didn't want to teach beginners."

"Well, the ad did say advanced latte class." Lauren tried to be fair. "Maybe he prefers baristas who are experienced."

"I think it's a good thing he didn't try to teach Judy and Frank tonight," Zoe said. "Because he might have discouraged them for life!"

CHAPTER 2

The next day, Tuesday, Lauren and Zoe opened the café right on the dot of 9.30 a.m.

Pale yellow walls complemented pine tables and chairs. An oak entrance door invited customers to come on in.

"I'm going to make swans and peacocks today," Zoe said as she stood behind the counter, waiting for their first customer.

"Me too." Lauren smiled at her.

"But what if it goes horribly wrong?" Zoe bit her lip.

"I'm sure our regulars won't mind a bit of wonkiness if you explain what you were trying to achieve," Lauren reassured her, wondering if she was right.

"Oh, I know!" Zoe's face brightened. "I'll make a latte for Ed."

"Good idea." Lauren stepped away from the espresso machine so Zoe could get started.

Ed was their pastry chef – a big, burly man who seemed to dislike small talk but made Danish like a dream. He started early and usually left mid-afternoon. Sometimes Lauren thought their customers came for Ed's pastries instead of her cupcakes and coffee, but since nearly everything sold out by the end of the day, it was a fortunate problem to have.

"Brrt?" Annie, her silver-gray tabby, trotted over to Lauren.

"We're waiting for our first customer." Lauren smiled down at the Norwegian Forest Cat.

Although Lauren had inherited the café from her grandmother and had turned it into a certified cat café, Annie seemed to think it was *her* café. When she and Annie had moved to Gold Leaf Valley after her grandmother's death, Annie had taken on the hostess role. She seemed to love seating the customers and had her favorite regulars.

The machine growled as Zoe extracted an espresso, the scents of cherry and cocoa filling the air. The wand hissed as she steamed the milk.

"Here goes," Zoe declared, tapping the jug on the counter and swirling it. She began to pour the milk into the latte mug, concentrating. "I did it!" She gazed at the mug a few seconds later, her face alight with excitement. "Look!"

Lauren peered over her shoulder. "Yes, you did!"

A heart shaped head and well defined wings and body.

"Brrt?" Annie asked.

"I made a swan, Annie." Zoe giggled. "Remember we went to latte art class last night?"

"Brrp." Annie seemed to nod by inclining her head slightly.

"Now I've made a picture of a swan on top of the coffee!"

"And she's going to give it to Ed to drink," Lauren added.

"Brrt!" Annie seemed to think that was a good idea.

"Look, Ed." Zoe pushed open the swinging doors into the kitchen. "I made you a latte!"

Lauren heard Ed grunting and Zoe's voice, but couldn't quite make out the actual words.

"He said it looked good." Zoe grinned as she came out of the kitchen. "And now

I'm going to make a peacock for our first customer."

"Who orders a coffee," Lauren said.

"Well, not many people order tea." Zoe frowned. "Or just want a bottle of water or juice."

Before she could say anything more, the front door opened.

"Hello, dears." An elderly woman wearing a green pants suit and black lace-up shoes leaned on her walking stick at the *Please Wait to be Seated* sign.

"Hi, Mrs. Finch." Lauren hurried to greet her.

"Brrt!" Annie scampered over to one of her favorite customers.

"Would you like a coffee, Mrs. Finch? Latte, cappuccino, mocha?" Zoe asked hopefully.

"I think I'd prefer a pot of tea this morning, dear," Mrs. Finch replied, peering at them through wire-rimmed spectacles.

"Oh." Zoe's face fell.

"Of course," Lauren said hastily. "Annie will seat you and we'll get your tea started. Would you like anything else?"

"Do you have any apple cake, Lauren?" Mrs. Finch asked. "I don't know why but I have a craving for it."

"No." Lauren hated disappointing her. "I'm sorry. I have cinnamon swirl, blueberry, and vanilla cupcakes today."

"Ed's pastries are nearly ready," Zoe chimed in. "But he's making apricot Danish and cherry pinwheels."

"Never mind, dears," Mrs. Finch murmured. "Just a pot of tea will do."

"Brrt," Annie said importantly, slowly leading the way to a small table near the counter. She seemed to know the senior couldn't walk quickly.

"I'll make it," Lauren told her cousin. She felt a little disappointed as well. She knew the secret to good latte art was to practice, just as Giovanni had told them last night. Hopefully it would be a busy day and she and Zoe would have plenty of opportunities to perfect their new skills.

Lauren took the pot of English Breakfast tea over to Mrs. Finch. Annie sat facing the elderly lady, talking her to her in a series of "brrps" and "brrts".

"I was just telling Annie about my trip to the library yesterday," Mrs. Finch said as Lauren set the teapot down. "I borrowed a book about a woman who runs an animal orphanage in Mongolia. Imagine that!"

"That sounds interesting." Zoe came over to the table.

"It is." Mrs. Finch nodded.

Lauren poured the tea.

"Thank you, dear." Mrs. Finch picked up the teacup with wobbly hands and took a sip. "Ah. That's better."

"I thought you'd switched to coffee," Zoe said.

"You're right, Zoe. But some days I still prefer a good cup of tea."

Recently, Lauren and Zoe had set up a pod machine for Mrs. Finch. Her son had given it to her as a gift, but she hadn't known how to use it until Lauren and Zoe had shown her. She'd been pleasantly surprised with the coffee capsules, and had changed from drinking strictly tea, to tea and coffee.

"Are you coming to knitting and crochet club this week, girls?" Mrs. Finch asked.

"Definitely." Zoe nodded. "I've only got a couple of rows to go and I'll have finished my scarf."

"That's wonderful." Mrs. Finch turned to Lauren. "How's yours coming along, dear?"

Lauren inwardly groaned. Her never-ending scarf knitted in garter stitch. At this rate, it would *never* be finished.

"It's getting there." *Eventually.* Lauren summoned a bright smile.

"Lauren hasn't had much time to work on it lately," Zoe said. "We've been busy with the café and last night we went to advanced latte art class."

"Brrt," Annie said knowingly. When they'd returned home last night, Zoe had told Annie all about it. By the time Lauren had slid into bed, Annie lying next to her, on top of the covers, there hadn't been much news left to share with her.

"I'm sure you'll be able to get some done on Friday night, Lauren." Mrs. Finch took another sip of her tea. "Zoe, what will your next project be?"

"I'm not sure yet," Zoe replied. She'd started knitting club, which had now become knitting and crochet club, a couple of months ago. There were four members, including Annie. "Today, I want to make as many swans and peacocks as possible." At Mrs. Finch's enquiring look, Zoe filled her in on their class last night.

"Goodness," Mrs. Finch said when Zoe ran out of breath. "This barista fellow sounds very interesting."

"Yes," Lauren replied. "He's won a lot of international awards and can do tons of different designs."

"I was so excited when Lauren and I decided to attend his class," Zoe added. "But I didn't realize he would be so – so—"

"Intense?" Lauren suggested.

"Exactly!"

The door opened with a whoosh, snagging Lauren's attention. Was it Mitch Denman? The detective had recently asked her out, but they hadn't settled on an actual time and place yet. He was busy with work, and the café kept her occupied.

A man in his fifties walked in. At first glance, Lauren thought it might be Frank from last night's class. But no. This man was taller and she couldn't spot a bald patch in his dark hair.

"I'll go." Zoe zoomed to the counter.

"Brrt." Annie hopped off her chair and trotted to the man.

Lauren watched him follow the cat, a quizzical look on his face as Annie led him to a table in the rear. Then she scampered back to Mrs. Finch.

The newcomer picked up a menu, and relaxed in his chair.

Zoe hurried over to him. They usually didn't take orders at tables, unless the customer was elderly, infirm, or harried.

"I think Zoe wants to practice her swans," Lauren told Mrs. Finch.

"Oh, I see." Mrs. Finch smiled.

"Brrt!"

Zoe strode to the counter, a grin on her face. The espresso machine growled as she set to work.

A couple of minutes later, Zoe stopped by Mrs. Finch's table.

"Look." She pointed to the mug she carried. "A swan!"

"That looks wonderful, dear," Mrs. Finch praised the design. "How clever!"

"Thanks." Zoe continued on to the new customer's table, setting down the latte with a flourish.

Lauren chatted to Mrs. Finch for a couple more minutes, then left her and Annie to continue their conversation.

"I can't wait for next week," Zoe told her as she joined her at the counter. "Wait until I show Giovanni my progress!"

The day passed swiftly. To Lauren's disappointment, Mitch didn't come in. At this rate, they would never find a time to even discuss going on their first date. But she did get the opportunity to make several swans, and to her relief they were just as good as her best effort the night before.

It was nearly five o'clock, closing time, when Mitch, lean and muscular in charcoal slacks and a pale blue dress shirt, strode through the door. Lauren's stomach fluttered as he approached the counter.

"Brrt?" Annie's ears pricked up as she trotted over to him.

"Hi." He smiled down at the cat. "I'm getting take-out."

"Brrt." It sounded as if she were chiding him.

"Hi," Lauren said, her tone a little breathless.

"Hi." Mitch's dark brown eyes warmed as he looked at her. "I'm sorry I haven't been around much lately – there's been a big case at work."

"Oh?" Mitch had investigated the two recent murders in the otherwise peaceful small town.

"Nothing that happened around here," he told her hastily. "In a neighboring town."

"Oh." Lauren relaxed slightly. She was too attracted to him to be fully at ease.

"Would you like a latte?"

"That would be great." He dug in his pocket for his wallet.

"On the house, remember?" She started grinding the beans. A few weeks ago, Mitch had mowed her lawn, and she'd promised him free coffee and cupcakes for a month.

"I thought we could talk about getting together. For our date."

Lauren's heart stopped for a moment.

"I'd like that," she replied shyly, for once finding the hissing of the milk wand intrusive instead of soothing.

"So, I was thinking, what about Friday night?"

"Friday?" She stared at him. Would Zoe be disappointed if she chose a date with Mitch over knitting and crochet club? Or would her cousin tell her to go for it?

"Yeah." He rocked back on his heels. "Unless you're busy. We can make it some other night—"

"No, no." She shook her head, sending her light brown hair flying around her face. "Friday is fine." She hoped Mrs. Finch and Annie wouldn't be too disappointed with her non-attendance.

"Great." His smile looked like it was tinged with relief. "There's an Italian restaurant in the next town – not where my case is," he added hastily. "We could go there."

"Okay." Her hand shook as she put the plastic lid on top of his latte.

"Seven o'clock?"

"Fine."

"I'll pick you up."

She stared after his departing figure, only realizing after a couple of minutes she'd forgotten to make a swan – or any type of art – on his latte.

CHAPTER 3

"About time!" Zoe cheered when Lauren told her the news. Her cousin had just come in from the kitchen, declaring everything was clean and tidy. "Don't worry about crochet club – I'll be able to finish my scarf and I'm sure Annie will keep us company."

"Brrt," Annie agreed, looking at Lauren with bright-eyed interest. At first, the cat hadn't seemed too keen on Mitch, but that might have been because he hadn't known how to interact with her. Until he'd started coming to the café, he hadn't had much experience with cats at all.

But it was as if Annie sensed Lauren's interest in the detective, and had decided to approve of Mitch. The fact that he had arrested two murderers in the recent past might have helped sway her opinion as well.

"Thanks, guys." Lauren sank down on the stool behind the counter. They'd just closed for the day. Ever since Mitch had entered the café, her legs had wobbled.

"You'll tell Mrs. Finch I'm sorry I can't make it, won't you?"

"Of course." Zoe grinned. "But I'm sure she'll be thrilled to hear you've gone on a date with Mitch. You'll have to tell us all about it when you get home."

"Brrt!"

They finished tidying the café, then walked through the private hallway that led to Lauren's cottage.

"What shall we do tonight?" Zoe flopped down on the sofa in the living room. "Nothing too strenuous. I think my arm needs a rest from latte art."

"I know what you mean," Lauren replied. "Maybe I'll get out my cookbooks and find a recipe for apple cake. I hated disappointing Mrs. Finch today when she asked for some."

"Good idea." Zoe jumped up. "I bet there's tons of different apple cakes you could make. Ooh, I know!" She glanced down at Annie who had joined them. "What about Norwegian Apple cake?"

"I've never heard of it," Lauren admitted. She narrowed her eyes. "Did you just make that up?"

"Yes," Zoe confessed cheerfully. "But I bet lots of countries have their own version of apple cake. The other day I saw a recipe for Somerset apple cake. I bet there's tons of others out there."

"I'll check my books." Lauren went over to the bookcase in the corner and pulled out a couple.

"I'll be able to find it faster online." Zoe fetched her laptop and sank onto the sofa. Annie hopped up next to her.

The sound of the keyboard clacking provided a backdrop to Lauren's rustling as she flicked through her baking books.

"Found it!" Zoe crowed.

"What's the point of digging out my books if you're going to find it quicker on the Internet?" Lauren sighed, then replaced the books on the shelves. Finding recipes online might be faster, but she usually enjoyed looking through her cookbooks. And deciding on an apple cake to experiment with would help take her mind off the fact she was going on her first date with Mitch in three days' time.

"You need apples, butter, sugar, flour, baking powder, nuts," Zoe read out the list of ingredients. "We should have all that."

"You're right." Lauren joined her cousin and Annie on the sofa.

"See?" Zoe handed her the laptop.

Lauren read through the recipe. It sounded easy and it had some glowing reviews.

"I'll make it on the weekend and we can see what it tastes like," she said.

"Awesome." Zoe grinned. "It's been a while since I've eaten apple cake."

"Brrp?" Annie asked, looking from the screen to Lauren.

"Yes, you can help if you'd like to." Lauren stroked Annie, her soft and silky fur like a caress on her fingers.

Annie wasn't allowed in the café kitchen for health reasons, but it was a different matter in their cottage.

"Brrt!" Annie sounded happy.

They decided to watch a rom-com on TV, but Lauren found it hard to concentrate. What would she wear on her date with Mitch? What would they talk about on the short drive to Zeke's Ridge? She hadn't been to that particular restaurant before, so she guessed they could discuss that. Before she could worry anymore about Friday night, her eyelids began to droop. It had been a busy day.

***

Lauren was determined to practice making peacocks the following morning. She also needed to check she had all the ingredients for the Norwegian Apple cake recipe Zoe had found online.

Perhaps she should make the cake before the weekend? If today was a slow day, she might feel like baking this evening – with Annie helping.

"Oh no," Zoe muttered as a woman entered the café right on 9.30. Tall, thin, and middle-aged, Ms. Tobin was their most difficult customer. But today, instead of her usual depressing brown, she wore a fawn skirt and top that looked more attractive.

"Brrt," Annie greeted the woman.

"Hello, Annie." What passed for a smile ghosted Ms. Tobin's lips. Something else that was out of character.

Annie led her to a table in the middle of the room.

"What is she carrying?" Zoe talked out of the side of her mouth.

"I think it's a tablet," Lauren replied. "Or an iPad."

"I can't remember her ever doing that before," Zoe said.

"I'll serve her."

Ms. Tobin usually found fault with something. Everything had to be just so. What surprised Lauren was that she kept coming back to the café.

"Oh, hello, Lauren." Ms. Tobin looked up from her device. Annie had already departed.

"What can I get you, Ms. Tobin?" Lauren asked politely. She knew from experience that Ms. Tobin expected table service, although she was neither elderly nor infirm.

"I'll have a large latte. What sort of cupcakes do you have today?"

"Lemon drizzle, vanilla, and triple chocolate," Lauren replied. The triple chocolate had been a recent creation of hers and had proven to be a bestseller.

"What about Ed's pastries?" Ms. Tobin inquired.

"Apricot Danish, and blueberry today." Lauren held her pencil, ready to write down the order.

"I'll have a triple chocolate cupcake," Ms. Tobin replied. "People have been telling me about them."

"They have?" Lauren asked quizzically. Mentally, she'd always tried to be fair to the woman, wondering if her unhappiness stemmed from a disappointing life, but she couldn't imagine her other regulars talking to Ms. Tobin about something like that.

"They're supposed to be delicious," Ms. Tobin replied, her thin mouth tilting upward at the corners. Was that her attempt at a smile?

"I hope you enjoy it." Lauren scratched out the order, then hurried back to the counter.

"Well?" Zoe demanded when Lauren slapped down the ticket on the counter.

"A large latte and a chocolate cupcake." For once, Ms. Tobin hadn't instructed her on how to make the latte.

"I'll make a swan – no, you make it," Zoe said, stepping away from the espresso machine. "That way, she can't criticize my design."

Lauren shook her head at her cousin's reasoning, and ground a double shot. Perhaps she shouldn't attempt a peacock on Ms. Tobin's coffee – but she could manage a swan, couldn't she?

"You plate the cupcake," she told Zoe. Ms. Tobin didn't like to be kept waiting, and since she was their only customer this morning, she would be sure to point that out to them if they took even one minute longer than usual.

Lauren concentrated on correctly aiming the nose of the milk jug into the latte mug. Pour, pour, wiggle, pour – she pulled through at the end with a small flourish.

"Awesome!" Zoe's eyes widened as she stared at the bird on the surface of the coffee. "You should take a photo – that's a really great one."

"You think?" Lauren smiled as she studied her art. "What would Giovanni say?"

"Bellissimo!" Zoe put on an Italian accent, then giggled.

"I'd better take it over to her." Lauren loaded up a tray and walked over to the table, not wanting to jostle the coffee.

"Thank you, Lauren." Ms. Tobin looked up as Lauren placed the tray on the table, her hand covering the screen of her tablet. "That cupcake looks delightful."

"It does? Thank you," Lauren tried to recover from the unexpected compliment. She passed the latte to the older woman.

"Oh, a swan!" Ms. Tobin glanced at Lauren. "Is this a new design?"

"Yes. Zoe and I learnt how to do it at class this week."

"It looks very nice," Ms. Tobin told her. "Keep up the good work, Lauren."

"Um – thank you." Lauren grabbed the tray and hurried back to the counter.

"Well?" Zoe hopped on one leg. "What did she say? I bet she found fault with it in some way."

"No. No, she didn't." Lauren sank down on a stool and recounted the conversation to her cousin.

"Whoa!" Zoe looked over at Ms. Tobin. "I think this is the first time she's been nice since you took over the café."

"I know." Lauren nodded.

Annie jumped down from her pink cat bed on the shelf and ambled over to Ms. Tobin. "Brrt?"

Zoe clutched Lauren's arm. "Annie's never done that before."

"True." Annie seemed to sense that while Ms. Tobin liked being escorted to a table, she didn't want any further interaction.

"Hello." Ms. Tobin peered down at the silver-gray tabby. "I'm writing an email." Her voice was low but Lauren could just make out the words.

"Brrp." Annie jumped up on the chair next to the woman, as if she wanted to hear more about it.

Ms. Tobin showed Annie the small screen. The cat pricked up her ears and looked at her quizzically.

"She hasn't even tried her cupcake," Zoe whispered to Lauren. "So it can't be the chocolate that's put her in a good mood."

"Do you think –" Lauren hesitated, knowing she shouldn't speculate – "do you think Ms. Tobin has a boyfriend – man friend – friend?" It sounded weird to call a man in his fifties or older a "boyfriend". She guessed that would be the age range Ms. Tobin would deem appropriate for herself – if she was interested in dating.

"No way!" Zoe shook her head. "She's so – so – sour."

"Not today," Lauren said softly.

Zoe drew herself up and straightened her shoulders. "If Ms. Tobin's got a boyfriend, then why can't I even get a date with someone?"

After her last attempt at internet dating had gone disastrously wrong, Zoe had channeled her energies into knitting and crochet.

"There's plenty of time." Lauren patted her cousin's shoulder. "You're only twenty-five."

"But I don't want to turn out like Ms. Tobin," Zoe whispered in anguish. To their knowledge Ms. Tobin had never been married.

Lauren took a step back and stared at her livewire cousin.

"There is no way that could happen. You have such a great attitude to life."

"Really?" Zoe's pixie bangs flopped against her forehead and her brown eyes grew misty. "You, too."

"Thanks." Lauren smiled at her cousin. She hadn't dated for a while before Mitch Denman had stepped into the café for the first time, reasoning it was better to be single than stuck in an unhappy relationship. But she'd always admired Zoe's zest to pursue what made her happy.

"Brrp."

Lauren glanced over at Ms. Tobin's table. Annie jumped off the wooden chair, sauntering back to her cat bed. Ms. Tobin watched her, a pleasant expression on her face, then her gaze dropped to her device and she began typing.

If Ms. Tobin was dating, it was certainly putting her in a good mood.

CHAPTER 4

Only one day to go until her date with Mitch. After a slow start, yesterday had turned out to be quite busy, so Lauren hadn't attempted making the Norwegian Apple cake.

"Maybe tonight," she told Annie as she unlocked the front door to the café Thursday morning.

"Brrt!" Annie's long whiskers twitched, the June morning sunshine glinting off them.

"Hi, there." A short, balding man stepped into the café a second later.

"Frank!" Lauren stared at him in surprise.

"Been practicing your latte art?" He grinned at her. "I've been doing it every day, using a little stick whizzer to foam the milk. Now I can make a tulip as well as a heart."

"That's great." Lauren walked behind the counter. "Zoe and I have been perfecting our swans."

"Can't wait to be able to do the more advanced stuff like that." He glanced down at Annie, who stared at him patiently. "Is this your cat?"

"Yes," Lauren replied. "If you'd like a table, she'll choose one for you."

"Really?" He eyed Annie skeptically. "I've never heard of that."

"It's Annie's thing." Lauren shared a special look with her.

"Brrt!" Annie agreed.

"I'd love to see it, but I was hoping to have a chat with you and Zoe."

"Oh?"

"Ed says the apple Danish will be ready in a few minutes." Zoe pushed open the swinging kitchen doors then skidded to a stop on the balls of her feet. "Sorry, I didn't realize we had a customer already."

"We met at latte art class. Zoe, right?" Frank moved from the *Please Wait to be Seated* sign to the counter.

"Oh, that's right." Zoe joined Lauren behind the counter. "You were with Judy."

"Nice lady." Frank nodded.

"Would you like a coffee?" Zoe asked. "I'll make a swan for you."

"What about a peacock?" Frank laughed.

Zoe looked doubtful. "I was going to practice those today."

"Me too," Lauren said.

"A coffee would be good. I'll have a regular latte." Frank scanned the counter, his gaze alighting on the half-full tip jar. "Do you get lots of tips here?"

"Sometimes," Zoe answered. "Why?"

He chuckled. "I've been checking out the local cafes, trying to see what makes them popular – and testing their coffee, of course. If I'm going to start a coffee blog, then I'll need to understand the biz."

"Oh?" Lauren exchanged a concerned glance with her cousin. Last month, a food critic and blogger had visited them and things hadn't turned out well for him.

"Yes, like tampers, and portafilters, the different types of coffee beans. And then there's home roasting of course, and the different flavor profiles you can achieve by getting to first crack or second."

"You seem to have picked up a lot of the lingo," Zoe commented.

"Brrp," Annie seemed to agree as she wandered over to her cat bed. Perhaps all the coffee talk wasn't interesting to her for once.

"Do you roast your own beans?" He leaned on the counter.

"No," Lauren replied, as the espresso shot poured into the mug.

"I've been reading up about it. Pretty easy, if you ask me. You can even use an air popcorn maker."

"Really?" Zoe asked over the hiss of the steam wand as Lauren foamed the milk.

"Yes. And people say their own beans taste better than buying freshly roasted coffee online."

"Which people?" Lauren frowned as she got the milk jug into position to attempt a peacock.

"Coffee forums," Frank replied. "And green coffee beans cost less than roasted beans."

"I didn't know that." Zoe turned to her cousin. "Did you?"

"Yes." Lauren didn't look up as she poured and wiggled.

"Why don't we roast our own beans, Lauren?" Zoe asked.

"Think of the money you could save," Frank added.

"Because we would need to roast a lot of coffee each week," Lauren replied. "And I've read you lose twenty percent volume from the green coffee beans when you roast them." She didn't need to be distracted right now. What if the peacock turned out to be a sloppy mess?

"I didn't know that, either." Zoe frowned.

Lauren pulled through the design with a little flourish. "There you go."

Either being distracted helped her latte art or she hadn't allowed the conversation to switch her focus. The peacock looked pretty decent, with a fanned-out tail.

"Thanks." Frank studied the art. "That's really good. I watched you make the latte and I'd love to try doing it myself. Amy made our espressos and steamed the milk at class and I took notes. What do you say I make the coffee for your next customer?"

Lauren and Zoe stared at each other for a second, their eyes wide.

"I'm afraid that's not possible," Lauren replied. "Insurance."

"Yeah, insurance," Zoe added. "You know."

"I get it." Frank nodded, then took a sip of his drink. "It's a shame to ruin such a nice pattern, but I was certainly curious about your coffee. It's great."

"Thanks," Lauren replied.

"You should try her cupcakes," Zoe said loyally. "And Ed's pastries. I can see if his apple Danishes are ready."

"Sounds good." Frank grinned.

Zoe vanished into the kitchen.

Lauren watched Frank take another sip of the latte and wondered what to say to him. She wished she'd been the one to check on the pastries.

"I think I'll buy an espresso machine," Frank said. "I'll need to anyway if I want to be an expert in latte art."

"Good idea," Lauren replied. "There are plenty on the market – manual, semi-automatic, and automatic."

"I'll have to do some research first," he said, picking up his cup again. "And then I'll roast my own beans."

"That should certainly be interesting," Lauren replied pleasantly.

The swinging kitchen doors swished as Zoe bustled into the café.

"All ready." She held a large tray of golden pastries, the filling glistening with sticky sumptuousness. The aroma of sweet apple filled the air.

"Mmm." Frank patted his slight paunch. "Can't wait to try one."

"Would you like to sit at a table?" Lauren asked. "Annie can show you to one."

"Why not?" Frank shrugged.

"Annie," Lauren called.

"Brrp?" Annie hopped down from her bed and ambled over to them.

"Could you choose a table for Frank, please?"

"Brrt," Annie said importantly. She glanced up at the man, then trotted towards the rear of the café.

Frank looked at Lauren and Zoe, as if wondering what to do next.

"Follow her," Zoe told him. "We'll bring your order."

"Okay." He followed the cat to the two-seater table, a look of disbelief on his face.

Lauren loaded up the tray, Zoe accompanying her.

"You two certainly have got a good gimmick." Frank's gaze followed the silver-gray tabby as she padded back to her bed.

"We don't like to think of it like that," Lauren informed him with a frown.

"If it was a gimmick, then we wouldn't take pride in our coffee and baked goods," Zoe added.

Frank took a bite of the Danish. A look of satisfaction crossed his face. "I can see why people come to your café."

"You should try Lauren's triple chocolate cupcake," Zoe said.

"Why not?" Frank shrugged in a *let's do it* way.

"I'll get it." Lauren hurried back to the counter. Should they charge Frank for his order or not? She felt a little awkward about it, especially with Zoe encouraging him to sample the sweet treats.

She plated the cupcake and walked back to the table, passing Annie in her cat bed. She seemed to be dozing.

Zoe sat at the table across from Frank.

"Amy really seems to know her stuff," he told Zoe as Lauren set down the cupcake. "She said she's been Giovanni's partner for a few years now."

"Business or romantic, or both?" Zoe asked curiously.

"Zoe!" Lauren murmured.

"She didn't say." Frank dug his fork into the large swirl of creamy cocoa colored ganache on top of the cupcake. "This looks good. Tastes good too," he mumbled a second later.

The entrance door opened, and Father Mike stood at the *Please Wait to be Seated* sign.

"We'll leave you to enjoy it." Lauren moved toward the counter.

"I was wondering if you were going to get more customers this morning." Frank attacked the cupcake with gusto, a grin on his face.

***

"I'm going to make Norwegian Apple cake tonight," Lauren stated as they closed the café that afternoon.

The last customer had left a few minutes ago, just before five o'clock.

"Brrt?" Annie's ears pricked up as she sauntered over to Lauren.

"Yes, you can help." Lauren smiled down at the cat.

It had been a moderately busy day. She'd had a chance to try some more peacocks – so had Zoe. But Zoe had become discouraged with her efforts and had gone back to making swans.

But every time she thought of tomorrow and her date with Mitch, her stomach had fluttered so hard she thought a kaleidoscope of butterflies would escape the confines of her stomach and fly around the room.

Baking would help take her mind off tomorrow night.

"Let's go." Zoe stacked her last chair. "The kitchen's clean."

"Good." Lauren smiled at her cousin. "I think I've got all the ingredients I need at home."

"But if you don't, I'll fetch what you need from here." Zoe grinned.

"Brrt!" Annie trotted toward the locked door that led to their private hallway.

"We're coming." Lauren followed the cat.

"There were a couple of paninis left over so I thought we could have them for dinner." Zoe held up a brown paper bag.

"Good idea."

"And maybe we can have Norwegian Apple cake for dessert!"

"I hope so."

"Brrt!" Annie's green eyes gleamed with anticipation.

"You can help make it, Annie, but I don't think it will be good for you to eat any," Lauren told her.

Once they were in the cottage, Lauren opened the laptop. Zoe had bookmarked the online recipe she'd found.

"I'll leave you two to it," Zoe said. "I'll be in the living room working on my scarf."

"Okay," Lauren replied absently, her mind already on the cake.

"Brrp?" Annie asked softly, jumping up on a kitchen chair and peering at the laptop screen.

"We need butter, eggs, milk, sugar, flour, baking powder, cinnamon," Lauren read out. "And apples and almonds. We should have all that here."

Lauren mixed up the batter.

"See?" She showed the mixture to Annie.

"Brrp?" Annie stuck her head into the bowl, peering at the creamy yellow batter.

"Annie!" Lauren scolded gently, trying not to giggle. Just as well this cake was for her and Zoe's consumption and not their customers'.

"Brrp!" Annie lifted her head out of the bowl, some of the mixture clinging to her whiskers. She narrowed her eyes and stared at the yellow goop, as if wondering how that had happened.

"Brrt!" She shook her head, tiny drops of batter flying through the air and landing on the kitchen floor.

"We'd better clean your whiskers." Lauren reached for a clean soft cloth and dampened it with water.

She gently wiped the gooey whiskers, Annie keeping still, as if she appreciated what Lauren was doing.

"There. All clean." Lauren kissed the top of Annie's head.

"Brrp." *Thank you.*

"You're welcome." Lauren and Annie gazed at each other, sharing the moment, before they both blinked at the same time, breaking the spell.

"Is it in the oven yet?" Zoe appeared in the doorway.

"Not yet. I have to add the apple and nuts."

Zoe sat down at the kitchen table, watching Lauren work. Her gaze landed on a small glob of batter on the floor. "I'll get that."

"Thanks."

Lauren exchanged a secretive glance with Annie.

A few minutes later, Lauren slid the cake into the oven.

"I can't wait to try it." Zoe grinned. "And while you were baking, I nearly finished my scarf!"

"That's great."

"Guess what I saw at lunch today on my phone!"

"What?" Lauren asked.

"Brrp?"

"Crocheted coffee cozies!"

"What are they?" Lauren furrowed her brow.

"You put them on your take-out coffee cup," Zoe told her. "There are tons of them on the handmade craft sites. And they look pretty easy to make. I'm going to make one after I finish my scarf – ooh, Mrs. Finch could help me find a simple pattern tomorrow night. I'll take the laptop with me."

"But you don't buy much coffee in a take-out cup." Lauren wondered if she was missing something.

"I know I get all the coffee I need from the café and here." Zoe gestured to the kitchen they were in. "But I'm going to sell my cozy."

"Sell it?" Lauren stared at her cousin.

"Why not? All I have to do is set up an account, take a photo of it, and boom! I'm going to buy a fancy button and sew it on the cozy." Zoe's face fell for a second. "Maybe Mrs. Finch could do that for me." Zoe was not known for her sewing. "And then make some money! This way, I won't have to raid my share of the tip jar if I want to treat myself before pay day."

"You know I can always give you an advance," Lauren offered.

"I know," Zoe replied with a smile. "But I think this will be fun to do. I might even finish making the whole thing tomorrow night at Mrs. Finch's!"

"That would be great." Lauren felt herself being swept along in her cousin's enthusiasm.

"But your date with Mitch will be even greater." Zoe giggled. "I can't wait to hear all about it when you come home. Annie and I will stay up."

"Brrt!" *Yes!*

"Okay," Lauren said good naturedly. If Mitch walked her to her front door at the end of the night, she'd have to remember to tell him they might have an audience of two.

***

Zoe declared the Norwegian Apple cake a hit. So did Lauren.

"I love the apples and the almonds in it." Zoe put down her fork with a clatter as she polished off her second piece. "I wonder if you could make a cupcake version?"

"I'll have to see if that will work." Although Lauren mainly made cupcakes, she did bake some full-size cakes for the café, and cut them into slices.

"You could make this tomorrow morning and see what the customers think." Zoe's eyes sparkled. "I hope Mrs. Finch comes in – she asked for apple cake the other day."

"Good idea." Lauren had already mixed up the batter for two cupcake offerings tomorrow, but hadn't decided on a third one. This would be the perfect solution.

"We're going to be busy tomorrow." Zoe stretched and yawned. "A new cake, crochet club, and your date with Mitch."

CHAPTER 5

First thing Friday morning, Lauren made a Norwegian Apple cake in the café's kitchen. She'd been so busy trying not to think about her date with Mitch that evening, that she hadn't given much thought about what to wear.

The realization hit her just as Ed arrived.

After grunting good morning to her, he rolled up his sleeves. She left him to work his pastry magic, keeping an eye on the time. She'd have to take the cake out of the oven in one hour.

"I wonder if Mitch will drop by for a latte," Zoe teased as Lauren entered the café area.

"I hope not," Lauren replied, immediately wishing she could unsay it. She always felt breathless and a little tongue-tied around him – what would she be like today?

She grabbed her cousin's arm. "I have no idea what to wear tonight."

"Your plum wrap dress?" Zoe suggested. "I think it goes really well with your light brown hair and hazel eyes."

"Thanks." Lauren smiled. That dress was one of her favorites, as it also seemed to flatter her curvy figure.

"And your black kitten heels," Zoe added.

"Brrt," Annie seemed to agree.

"Okay." Lauren nodded.

When Lauren checked on the cake, it was ready to come out of the oven. Slices of cinnamon dusted apples decorated the top.

"That looks just as good as last night's cake." Zoe came up behind her in the kitchen. "Look, Ed."

Ed looked up from the pastry he was shaping.

"New recipe?" he asked.

"Yes," Lauren replied.

"We'll save you a piece," Zoe told him.

"Thanks." He smiled briefly, then returned his attention to the dough.

"I'll go and open up." Zoe zipped from the kitchen.

Lauren set the cake on a cooling rack and joined her cousin in the café. Ed didn't even seem to notice her departure.

"Hi Molly," Lauren heard her cousin greet their first customers. "Hi, Claire."

"Annie!" The blonde toddler in the stroller waved to the tabby who trotted over to the mother and daughter.

"Hi." Lauren smiled at the athletic mother, and her little girl Molly.

"Brrp." Annie looked up at them expectantly.

"Table, pwease." Molly beamed at the cat.

"Brrt!" Annie led them to a four-seater table in the middle of the room.

"I just love coming here," Claire told them. "And so does Molly."

"We love that you love it here." Zoe grinned.

The mother and daughter duo were among their favorite customers – and Annie's. Molly and Annie seemed fascinated with each other.

"I'd love a mocha this morning," Claire said. "And I know Molly would like a babycino."

"I'll get that started." Zoe hurried behind the counter.

"Which cake should I try today?" Claire asked.

Lauren glanced over at Annie. Molly was stroking her very gently, using 'fairy pats.' The feline seemed to lap up the attention.

"I've got a new cake you could try. Can you eat apples and almonds?" Lauren was aware that not everyone could eat nuts. She'd have to tell Zoe to mention the almonds to anyone who ordered the apple cake.

"Yes." Claire looked interested.

"Great." Lauren scratched out the order. "I'll surprise you."

"Can't wait." Claire smiled.

Lauren headed to the kitchen. By now, the cake should be cool enough to slice.

Ed thumped away with more dough, the pastry tins on the countertop rattling with the movement. He didn't seem to notice Lauren as she cut the cake into neat pieces.

She carried the tray out into the café and slid it in the glass case.

"It looks awesome." Zoe briefly looked up from the mocha she was making.

"Going for a peacock?" Lauren asked.

"Yep." The tip of Zoe's tongue peeked out as she frowned in concentration, pouring micro foam into the coffee cup.

A few seconds later, Zoe grinned. "I did it! Well, sort of." She showed Lauren the mug.

A smudgy peacock with most of its tail decorated the surface.

"Almost," Lauren encouraged.

"It's better than my efforts yesterday," Zoe said. "Whoops – I almost forgot Molly's order."

"I'll take the mocha over." Lauren didn't like to keep her customers waiting, especially for hot beverages.

"Thanks." Zoe spooned the left-over milk froth from Claire's drink into an espresso cup, dusted it liberally with chocolate powder, and added two marshmallows, pink, and white, to the side of the saucer.

Lauren added a slice of her new cake to the tray and headed toward Claire's table, aware of Zoe following her with the babycino.

"That looks interesting." Claire smiled as Lauren and Zoe set down the order.

"Cino!" Molly looked up from patting Annie and smacked her lips in anticipation.

"Careful now," Claire told her daughter, pushing the small cup and saucer toward her.

"Don't give Annie any," Lauren said. "Chocolate and marshmallows aren't good for her."

Molly pouted, and Lauren was sure Annie did the same.

"Bear." The toddler pulled a small brown teddy bear out of her stroller and held him over the espresso cup. "Bear have."

"I need this." Claire gazed at the surface of her drink. "Is that a peacock?"

"Yes," Zoe replied. "What do you think?"

"I've never seen one before, that's for sure."

"It needs a bit of work," Zoe admitted.

"I certainly couldn't make something like this," Claire admitted.

Lauren and Zoe told her about the advanced latte class they'd attended earlier that week.

"And we're going back next Monday," Lauren finished.

"For the makeup class. Except this time the beginners will get the famous barista, and we'll get Amy."

"Who sounds very nice from what the others have told us," Lauren said.

"I don't think she'll shout at us, anyway." Zoe nodded. "That might be a good thing."

"You'll have to tell me all about it next week," Claire said. She spooned up a mouthful of froth. "I hate having to destroy your picture."

"It's okay," Zoe assured her. "Enjoy it."

***

The day passed far too slowly. Every time someone stepped into the café, Lauren looked up, wondering if it would be Mitch. But no. She didn't know if that was good or not. She'd hadn't seen him since he'd asked her out to dinner. Was he still super busy at work?

By the time five o'clock rolled around, she couldn't wait to lock up and have a warm, soothing shower, then get ready for her date.

"What time is Mitch picking you up?" Zoe asked as she stacked the chairs on the table.

"Seven o'clock," Lauren replied.

"I can clean up here," Zoe said. "You go and get ready."

"Brrt," Annie agreed, looking up from her cat bed.

"Okay." Lauren picked up her phone and headed toward the private hallway. "Thanks."

She felt guilty leaving Zoe and Annie to close up, but she didn't want to rush around and be a harried mess when Mitch picked her up. At least, she didn't want to look like one.

Once inside the cottage, Lauren took a shower, washed her hair, and got dressed, taking Zoe's advice on the wrap frock and kitten heels.

By the time Zoe and Annie entered the cottage, Lauren was deciding how much makeup to wear.

"Maybe all you need is some lip color and mascara," Zoe advised from Lauren's bedroom door. "Mitch is used to seeing you without much makeup."

"That's true." Lauren made a face at her reflection. She'd never seen the need to wear much, if any, makeup while working in the café. She didn't want it steaming off her face when she was busy at the espresso machine.

"Brrt." *Yes.*

"Okay." Lauren applied the minimal makeup, hoping she wouldn't make a mess with the mascara.

"Are you going to be okay taking Annie to crochet club?" she asked once she was finished.

"Yep." Zoe nodded. "You want to go to Mrs. Finch's tonight, don't you?" She bent down to the cat.

"Brrt!"

"You'll have to wear your harness," Lauren warned.

A soft sigh that sounded suspiciously like a grumble came from Annie.

"We'll have a nice walk to crochet club," Zoe told Annie.

Mrs. Finch lived around the block, a pleasant stroll on an early summer evening.

"Brrp," Annie replied, looking a little more cheerful.

"We'll wait until Mitch picks you up, and then Annie and I will leave."

"Sounds like a plan." Lauren tried to smile but her facial muscles suddenly felt stiff. She checked her watch. Fifteen minutes to go.

"Annie and I better eat our dinner." Zoe glanced at Lauren. "Do you want anything?"

"Maybe a glass of water." Perhaps what she really needed was wine. Just a sip. But they didn't have any.

"Okay." Zoe headed down the hallway.

"Brrp?" Annie padded into the bedroom and jumped up on the bed.

Lauren sank down next to her.

"I'm okay." She stroked Annie's soft, silky gray fur. "Just a little nervous."

"Brrp." Annie bunted Lauren's palm.

"I hope dinner with Mitch goes well."

"Brrp," Annie replied encouragingly.

"Thanks." Lauren smiled at the feline. "You've made me feel better."

"Brrt," Annie replied softly. *Good.*

Lauren and Annie went to the kitchen.

"Here's your dinner, Annie." Zoe tapped her foot next to Annie's pink dish. "Chicken in gravy – yum."

Annie investigated the offering, her plumy tail waving.

"What are you having?" Lauren asked her cousin.

"Tuna sandwich." Zoe slapped a piece of whole wheat bread on top of the fish chunks and cut it in half. "Mrs. Finch and I will probably have a coffee from her pod machine."

Lauren suddenly wished she was going with Zoe to Mrs. Finch's instead of on her date. *It's just nerves,* she told herself.

Zoe cocked her head. "He's here!"

"He is?"

"I just heard a car pull up."

Since they were in the back of the cottage and the street was at the front of the house, Zoe's ears must have been finely attuned.

"How do I look?"

"Gorgeous." Zoe winked.

Ding dong.

Lauren's knees wobbled as she headed toward the front door. She pulled it open.

"Hi." Mitch smiled at her. Wearing slate gray slacks and a navy dress shirt, he looked just as attractive as ever. Maybe more so tonight. Because he was there, at her house. Going on a date with *her*.

"Hi," she managed, gripping onto her little black clutch purse so hard she was sure she would leave fingernail indentations.

"Are you ready?" he asked. "You look great."

"Thanks. Yes, I'm ready."

"We've got a 7.30 reservation for dinner."

Lauren nodded, stepping out onto the porch and shutting the door behind her.

"Let's go." She managed a smile.

CHAPTER 6

Lauren's date went well, if she didn't count her nerves kicking in. She succeeded in making small talk about the café on the way to the Italian restaurant in Zeke's Ridge.

Once there, the hostess showed them to their table immediately, and for a few minutes she was able to focus on the menu instead of *him*.

The food was delicious – they shared an order of bruschetta, topped with ripe cherry tomatoes, then Lauren enjoyed mushroom risotto, while Mitch had the chicken parmesan. During dinner Mitch revealed to her that he was settling into small town life.

"Where did you move from?" Lauren asked while they waited for dessert to arrive.

"Sacramento," he replied. "But I needed a change and thought Gold Leaf Valley sounded perfect – I can visit Sacramento whenever I need to."

That conversation led to Lauren telling him about her and Zoe's latte art class last week.

"We'll be going back for another class on Monday night," she finished.

"Will you make me a swan next time I come into the café?" he asked.

"Deal."

His dark brown eyes warmed as he looked at her. The butterflies returned to her stomach full force. Only the tiramisu arriving broke the spell.

Later, when Mitch drove her home, she remembered that Zoe and Annie were going to wait up for her.

"What's your cousin up to tonight?" he asked as he parked outside her cottage.

She couldn't help it – she giggled.

"Probably peeking through the window."

He looked amused as she told him about Zoe and Annie going to crochet club, and then waiting up for her.

"I'll walk you up." He accompanied her up the three steps to the porch.

"Thank you for dinner," she said as they stood facing each other at the front door. The yellow glow of the porch light shone down on them in the twilight. Zoe must have turned it on.

"My pleasure." He smiled down at her. He took a step closer, and she held her breath.

The moment was broken when he hesitated, then took a step back. Lauren looked at the front door and the window next to it.

She couldn't see a furry face peeking out, or her cousin. Unless they were hiding behind the drapes.

"I'll come in for a swan latte as soon as I can," he told her.

"Okay."

"Good night."

"Good night." They gazed at each for a long second, then Mitch strode down the steps towards his car.

***

"How was it?" Zoe and Annie ambushed Lauren as soon as she stepped inside the cottage.

"Good," Lauren replied.

"Only good?" Zoe teased.

"Brrt?" Annie looked up at her enquiringly.

"Okay." Lauren took a deep breath. "It was great. Apart from you two spying on us just now."

"Me? Spying?" Zoe placed her hand on her heart and widened her eyes.

"Brrt?" Annie looked the picture of innocence as well.

Zoe's giggle ruined the effect.

"Okay, you caught us. I tried not to, but I – we – gave in to temptation. Didn't we, Annie?" Zoe looked down at her.

"Brrt." *Yes.*

"We were behind the curtain in my bedroom," Zoe added.

"I knew it!" Lauren shook her head good-naturedly.

"It's a shame he didn't kiss you."

"Maybe he didn't want an audience."

"I – we – promise we won't do it again."

"Brrt." *Yes.*

***

Lauren, Annie, and Zoe spent a pleasant weekend together.

To Lauren's disappointment, Mitch didn't stop by the café on Saturday morning. But that afternoon, she tried to push the thought out of her mind as she made Norwegian Apple Cake, this time as cupcakes.

"This totally works," Zoe mumbled through her second sample, standing in the cottage kitchen. "And I love how you have sliced apple on top and a walnut." They only had walnuts left in the pantry.

"They do look pretty good," Lauren replied as she looked at the remaining eight cupcakes.

"Brrt!"

Annie had 'helped' her again with her baking, but this time she hadn't stuck her head in the bowl to investigate the batter.

"I bet Mitch will love these," Zoe teased.

"We'll see." Lauren blushed.

"I haven't shown you my coffee cozy!" Zoe hurried to her bedroom and came back with a brown paper bag. "Look!" She pulled out a small piece of mostly neat purple crochet. "It's the double crochet stitch. Mrs. Finch said it's coming along nicely."

"Did you finish your scarf?" Lauren asked as she turned over the woolen sleeve in her hands. She could see how this piece could slip over a to-go coffee cup.

"Yes, it's done!" Zoe beamed. "I can't wait for Fall when I can start wearing it."

"That's great."

"Brrt!"

"Now I just need to buy a fancy button for this coffee cozy and attach it, and sew up the sides. And look, Mrs. Finch helped me attach this yarn loop that will slip over the button and will hold the cozy in place on the cup."

"When are you going to buy the button?"

"On Monday. I thought I'd check out the handmade shop here." Zoe wrinkled her brow. "I should have chosen a button when I bought the yarn."

"You'll have plenty of time to do that and sew it on before latte class," Lauren said encouragingly.

"That's what I thought." Zoe grinned at her.

Zoe told her all about selling on one of the handcraft sites, until Lauren was certain she could open an account on there herself. But what would she sell? Not her red scarf, which she was still knitting. She'd leave the crafty stuff to her cousin, and focus on her baking and latte art designs.

On Sunday, Lauren and Zoe went to church – they hadn't been for a while. To her disappointment, she didn't see Mitch there, and she couldn't help wondering what he was doing right now.

They relaxed at home in the afternoon, Lauren knitting a few rows of her scarf before switching to a chick lit novel, trying to keep her thoughts off Mitch. Had he thought of kissing her on Friday night? Or had she been mistaken?

The café was closed on Mondays, but that didn't deter Zoe.

"I'd better practice my peacocks." She bounced into the cottage kitchen on Monday morning.

"Good idea." Lauren looked up from crunching her granola.

"Brrp?" Annie asked.

"You can watch us, Annie." Zoe grinned.

"But I thought you wanted to work on your crochet cozy."

"I will," Zoe assured her. "But I thought I could put in an hour of latte art practice first."

"Okay." Lauren nodded. "I'll practice with you."

"But we have to be careful not to do too much," Zoe mused. "Because I don't want to wear out my pouring arm before class tonight."

"True."

After breakfast, they walked down the private hallway to the café.

"Sometimes I think it's awesome having the café to ourselves." Zoe turned on the espresso machine.

"I know what you mean." Lauren glanced around the room. The pine chairs were stacked on the matching tables, and the whole space seemed empty without their customers.

Lauren and Zoe ended up putting in nearly two hours of practice, the espresso machine working overtime as Annie 'supervised'.

"I nearly did it that time!" Zoe crowed, gazing at her almost fully defined peacock. "I can't wait to show Giovanni tonight."

"Except we won't be studying with him," Lauren reminded her. "Amy will be teaching us."

"That's right." Zoe's expression fell.

"Maybe he'll check our designs sometime during class." Lauren attempted to cheer her up.

"At least he won't have a chance to shout at me if I'm not in his group." Zoe looked on the bright side.

Lauren did some grocery shopping while Zoe visited the handmade shop, buying a large ruby and gold colored button. They stopped in to see Mrs. Finch, Annie giving her a special hello. The elderly lady assured them she was fine, and that she would visit them tomorrow when the café was open.

Zoe crocheted her coffee cozy that afternoon. They had an early dinner at home, before driving to Sacramento.

"I wonder if everyone will be there tonight," Zoe mused.

"Why wouldn't they be?" Lauren crinkled her brow.

"I don't know – because they don't like Giovanni?"

"I think you're the one who doesn't like him," Lauren observed.

Zoe sighed. "Yeah – maybe. I thought he'd be a bit more patient with us – me."

"You're certainly qualified to be in the advanced class," Lauren told her.

"I just got a slight vibe that he didn't like me." Zoe frowned.

It was unusual that someone didn't like Zoe. She was fun and lively, and although she could be a little thoughtless at times, her heart was in a good place.

"Maybe he doesn't like anyone," Lauren said. "Apart from Amy."

"Yes, what is the deal with them?" Zoe tapped her lip. "Are they involved romantically or just partners in the cafe? Frank didn't know."

"I have no idea," Lauren replied. "It's really none of our business, though. We won't see them again after tonight."

"Yeah, I guess so." Zoe puffed out a breath.

They arrived at the coffee shop where the class was held.

"It looks like Frank is here already." Lauren pointed out his black compact car as she parked near it.

"And there's Judy's station wagon." Zoe gestured a little way down the street.

"We're not late, are we?" Lauren turned off the engine.

Zoe checked her watch. "No. We've got five minutes to spare."

The maple and white exterior seemed welcoming as they trooped into the café. The large plate glass windows glinted in the summer evening sunshine.

"Oh, good." Judy beamed at them. "We wondered if you were coming back."

"Of course," Lauren said.

"It's just that you're both so skilled already," Judy said.

"I can't wait to learn from Giovanni tonight." Frank rubbed his hands together.

"I wish I was," Casey, Judy's teen daughter, muttered.

"Oh, honey, you're so clever with all of this." Judy turned to the rest of them. "She's been practicing all week and her swans and peacocks are amazing!"

"Oh, Mom." Casey glowered and blushed at the same time.

"I should have practiced more," Zoe whispered to Lauren.

"Me too."

"Now a teenager is better than me."

"We'll see." Lauren gave her cousin an encouraging smile.

"I've got a great idea!" Judy rummaged in her capacious cream handbag. "Let's all swap phone numbers. It might be fun to get together one day and talk about our progress."

"Sure." Lauren dug out her phone. Judy seemed like a nice lady.

"I visited Lauren and Zoe's café last week." Frank held out his phone. "Impressive setup."

"Thanks." Zoe looked at him in surprised appreciation.

"If you like cats, you should go and visit," he told Judy and Casey.

"Ooh, I love cats." Judy beamed. "But my husband's allergic."

"That's a shame," Lauren said sympathetically. Sometimes she had trouble remembering what her life had been BA – Before Annie.

They'd just exchanged numbers with each other, apart from Casey, who'd declined, when Amy stepped into the room.

"Hello, everyone."

"Where's Giovanni?" Frank frowned.

"He'll be here in a minute," Amy looked down at her clipboard. "I'll have Lauren, Zoe, and Casey in my group tonight, and Judy and Frank will study with Gio."

"Can't wait." Frank rubbed his hands together.

Judy looked as if she could definitely wait – had she noticed the way Giovanni had been critical of Zoe's efforts last week?

Lauren's group moved to one end of the long espresso machine while Judy and Frank moved to the other end.

"I am here!" Giovanni burst into the room, just as good-looking as last week. He wore black slacks and a white polo t-shirt. "Good, you are all ready. Amy, have you told them what they are learning tonight?"

"I thought I'd leave that to you," Amy replied with a smile.

"I can do a heart," Judy said. "I've been practicing with my daughter. Of course, she's much better than me."

"That is good." Giovanni managed to sound like he almost believed it. "And you –" he narrowed his eyes, as if searching his memory "—Frank?"

"I can do a heart and a tulip," Frank boasted. "I've bought myself an espresso machine and I've been practicing nonstop."

Lauren and Zoe glanced at each other. That had been quick. Frank had visited them last week and had spoken about researching the various machines on the market.

"He must have stayed up all night reading espresso machine reviews," Zoe muttered to her.

Giovanni frowned at Zoe.

"We shall see, both of you." He looked at Judy and Frank. "Tonight, the advanced class will be learning bleeding hearts. Amy will teach them. But first, show me how much you have all learned from last week."

Amy smiled at Lauren, Zoe, and Casey. "Giovanni wants you to create a swan, and then a peacock. After that, I'll explain how to pour a bleeding heart."

"Cool," Casey murmured.

"You will make me a heart." Lauren heard Giovanni's voice at the other end of the counter. "I shall see how good you really are."

"No problem." Frank sounded confident.

The espresso machine growled and hissed as Lauren and Zoe made espresso shots for themselves and Casey.

After they steamed the milk, they set to work, the room quiet apart from Giovanni's mutters. Lauren was curious to find out what was going on in the beginner's group, but she needed to concentrate on her own art.

"That's very good, Lauren." Amy smiled at her approvingly. "A great swan, and a decent peacock. Giovanni was right last week when he said you have a good grasp of latte art."

"Thank you." Lauren's cheeks heated at the compliment.

"Good work, Zoe." Amy checked Zoe's art. "Your peacock needs some more definition on its tail but otherwise it's pretty decent. And your swan is good."

"Thanks!" There was a relieved look on Zoe's face.

"Casey, that is excellent," Amy praised the teen. "You could definitely enter barista competitions with that kind of quality."

"Awesome!" Casey murmured.

"She didn't say that to us," Zoe whispered to Lauren.

"I know," Lauren whispered back. "But her mom said she did a ton of practicing."

"Maybe we should have practiced more." Zoe sounded a little glum.

"Yeah." Lauren nodded.

"No talking!" Giovanni clapped his hands as he called the class's attention. "I almost forget to tell you. Today, we received a magnificent shipment of coffee beans. They are bellisimo!" He kissed his fingers. "You have never tried a milk-based espresso until you have tasted these beans. And," he paused, as if wanting them to recognize the significance of the moment, "you have the opportunity to buy a bag after class."

"Definitely!" Frank's eyes lit up. "I'm not really impressed with the beans I've bought so far. They're really bitter."

"You did not buy them from the supermarket, did you?" Giovanni asked.

"No." Frank shook his head. "I ordered them online and paid extra for fast shipping. What a disappointment."

"These beans were only roasted five days ago," Giovanni assured them. "You will not be sorry you bought them. If you are, bring them back and I'll give you a refund."

"We should get some." Zoe nudged Lauren.

"Yes." Lauren nodded. She noticed Giovanni hadn't mentioned the price. She hoped she had enough cash to cover the purchase, otherwise she'd have to put it on her credit card.

"What size are the bags?" Casey asked.

Giovanni's gaze zeroed in on her. "Twelve ounces."

"We should get some, Mom."

Judy nodded.

"We can arrange this after class," Amy cut in. "I think we should get back to latte art now."

Giovanni looked like he wanted to disagree, but instead turned to Frank and inspected his design.

The next hour passed swiftly. Amy might not have been a world-famous barista, but she was skilled, and her patient teaching style made Lauren glad she and Zoe were taking the class. Even Casey lost some of her sullenness and seemed to blossom under Amy's praise.

"I did it," Lauren murmured. She'd forgotten all about Giovanni teaching Judy and Frank. Immersed in perfecting her bleeding heart, she'd tuned out everything else. The base pour was similar to the swan's body, then she made a tulip shape which she turned into a heart. This design required a lot of control.

"Let me see." Zoe peeked over her shoulder. "Yes, you did! Why can't I do that?" She glanced down at her effort, a wonky heart on a bed of ripples.

"How are you girls going?" Amy approached them. "Oh, Lauren, that is very good. Casey, come and see what Lauren's achieved."

"Cool," Casey muttered, looking impressed for a second as she studied Lauren's pattern on the crema.

"This is exactly the sort of definition I'm looking for," Amy continued.

"I'm going to try again." Casey squared her shoulders.

Lauren watched the teen extract an espresso from the large machine, steam the milk, and then start pouring. Her technique was good, and Lauren was sure Casey would master bleeding hearts by the time class finished that night.

Half an hour later, Amy called for their attention.

"Thank you, everyone. I think we're finished for the night."

"Already?" Zoe looked surprised at the announcement.

"I have a little surprise for everyone." Amy smiled. "I'll be back in a jiffy."

Lauren and Zoe swapped intrigued glances with Judy, Casey, and Frank. Giovanni looked annoyed.

"I did a bleeding heart, Mom," Casey told Judy.

"That's wonderful, honey." Judy beamed at her daughter.

"How about you?" Casey asked.

Lauren thought that was the most Casey had said all night.

"I've been concentrating on hearts. I don't think I'm ready to start on tulips yet." Judy looked a little downhearted.

"I worked on rosettas tonight," Frank boasted. "They're pretty good, too. Right, Giovanni?"

"Yes," Giovanni replied. He seemed a little distracted.

"I wanted to thank everyone for attending." Amy strode into the classroom, carrying a rectangular cake covered in white frosting and pink fondant flowers. "And to apologize for last week's mix-up again."

"There is no need—" Giovanni started.

"Yes, there is." Amy held his gaze for a moment – there was a steeliness in her expression that Lauren hadn't noticed before. "So I thought we could all have a slice of cake before we leave."

"How wonderful!" Judy's gaze fastened on the delicious treat.

Amy cut the cake into even pieces with a sharp knife. She'd even provided plates, forks, and a stack of white paper napkins.

"Dig in, everyone."

"Mmm," Zoe mumbled around a mouthful. "Just about as good as yours."

"It is really nice." The vanilla crumb and frosting along with the extra sweetness of a fondant flower seemed exactly the right touch to end the evening. The taste of vanilla reminded her of Mitch and how much he liked her vanilla cupcakes.

They chatted with the others while they ate.

"It's a shame we can't have a latte with those amazing coffee beans Giovanni told us about," Frank said when he'd finished his treat. "It would have complimented the cake perfectly."

"You'll have to make yourself a coffee when you get home," Zoe suggested. "Which machine did you end up buying?"

Frank told them all about his new espresso machine. Out of the corner of her eye, Lauren saw Judy speak to Amy, and then the two of them headed into a room off the main café area, carrying the empty plates and the remainder of the cake. Were they going to the kitchen?

Giovanni had waved away Amy's offer of cake and was now shutting down the espresso machine. Was he hinting it was time to leave?

Lauren looked at her practical white plastic watch. "It's after 8.30," she told Zoe.

"We'd better go."

They said goodbye to Frank and Casey.

"You should check out the café I work at," the teen told them.

"Maybe we will," Zoe teased.

"I guess we'd better say goodbye to Giovanni," Lauren murmured.

"I guess." Zoe sounded reluctant.

But before they could approach him, the Italian clapped his hands.

"Everyone, it is time to leave. Class is over." He looked around the room. "Where are Amy and Judy?"

"I saw them go in there." Lauren gestured toward the room she'd seen them enter.

"Ah, the kitchen." He nodded. "I shall tell them." He strode off.

"Good luck with your coffee blog," Lauren told Frank.

"Thanks. And good luck with your café. I might drop by there again."

"No worries," Zoe's voice was cheerful.

"See you later." Casey nodded to Lauren and Zoe.

"Well, that was advanced latte art class," Zoe said as they walked out of the café and toward their car. The golden sky was streaked with pink.

"I'm glad we went."

"I think your bleeding heart was better than Casey's." Zoe commented. "I'll have to practice mine – a lot."

They got into Lauren's car and she started the engine.

"Oh no!" She turned to her cousin. "We forgot about the coffee beans."

"Oh, yeah!" Zoe snapped her fingers. "And Giovanni made them sound *amazing*."

"But he seemed to forget about selling them to us at the end of class," Lauren said.

"I think we should go back and buy some." Zoe unbuckled her seatbelt.

"Okay." Lauren checked her watch. "I hope it doesn't take too long, though. Annie might be cross if we're late home."

"Uh-huh."

They hurried back to the café. The entrance door was still unlocked and the lights were on inside.

But there was no one around in the main café area.

"Frank's car is still outside." Zoe frowned.

"Maybe they're all in the kitchen," Lauren suggested. "Judy's station wagon is out there, too."

"What if there's an office and that's where they're buying the coffee beans?"

"Let's find out." Lauren led the way to the kitchen. "We should check here first."

She poked her head into the kitchen, which had gleaming equipment.

"There must be an office somewhere." Zoe repeated.

A long hallway led off the café area. It was brightly lit, but Lauren felt a prickle of – what? Trepidation?

"Do you think we should go down there?" She stopped in her tracks.

Zoe halted as well. "What?"

"Listen."

The hallway was quiet. In fact, Lauren hadn't heard any noise since they'd walked back into the café.

"They're probably buying up all the coffee beans in Giovanni's office. That's why we can't hear anyone." Zoe forged down the hall. "And if we don't hurry, we'll miss out."

Lauren sighed and started after her cousin.

Another corridor opened up on her right. She glanced down it, then froze.

A pair of feet stuck out from a doorway.

CHAPTER 7

"Zoe!" Lauren's heart hammered.

"What?" Zoe looked back over shoulder impatiently. There must have been something amiss in Lauren's expression because Zoe hurried back to her.

Lauren's finger trembled as she pointed at the black shoes. Were they attached to legs – and a body?

"Oh no!"

Zoe's reaction snapped Lauren out of her daze. They both ran towards the feet. A man's body lay face down in what appeared to be a walk-in store room.

"Should we turn him over?" Zoe asked, her expression pale.

"I think so. What if he's still alive?"

Lauren took a deep breath, then placed her hand on the man's shoulder. He wore a white t-shirt. Her gaze drifted down. Black slacks. It wasn't …

"I'll help you." Zoe bent down and placed her hand next to her cousin's.

They managed to turn him onto his back.

"It's Giovanni!" Zoe stared at the man.

"And I think he's dead."

A knife covered in white frosting was stuck in his chest, a pink fondant flower smeared on his t-shirt. Blood pooled around the wound. His brown eyes were open as if he still stared in surprise at his assailant. Lauren looked away from his frozen expression and hoped she wasn't going to be sick.

"I'm calling 911." Lauren grabbed her phone from her bag and punched the buttons.

"Hello?" Amy's voice sounded down the hall. "Is that you, Gio?"

Lauren and Zoe looked at each other with wide eyes.

"Um, no." Zoe called out. "It's me and Lauren."

"Have you seen Gio?" Amy rounded the corner and approached them. "He said he was going to get the coffee beans from the storeroom after he finished his phone call." She waved a hand toward the small room were Giovanni lay.

The operator's voice came on the other end of the line, and Lauren focused on the conversation while keeping her gaze fixed on Zoe and Amy.

"Gio!" Amy kneeled beside him, her face stricken. "No!"

"I don't think you should get so close," Zoe warned. She touched Amy's shoulder, but the other woman shook her off.

"What happened?"

Lauren ended her phone call. "We mustn't let anyone else near him," she told Zoe.

Her legs wobbled and she desperately wanted to sit down.

"Amy." She tried to snag the woman's attention. "The authorities are on their way."

"Did you—" Amy turned a tear-stained face toward them. "What am I going to do?"

"He was like this when we found him a couple of minutes ago," Zoe told her.

"We forgot about buying the coffee beans. That's why we came back," Lauren added.

"Amy?" Frank's voice sounded down the hall. "Is there a problem? I can come back another time for the receipt."

"Frank wanted a receipt for his coffee beans," Amy turned to them. "I was going to write one out for him as the register is closed."

"Of course he wants a receipt," Zoe muttered.

Frank rounded the corner. "There you are – oh!"

"Yes. Oh." Tears slid down Amy's cheeks.

"What's going on?" Judy came into view. Casey tagged behind her. "I told you to stay in the office, honey." She turned to chide her daughter.

"I didn't want to stay there alone." Casey looked a little unsure of herself for once.

"Don't look." Lauren blocked their view.

"Are you sure he's dead?" Frank leaned over the body.

"Yes, we're sure." Zoe snapped. "And you're contaminating the crime scene."

Lauren looked at her cousin. It wasn't like Zoe to act like that.

"Sorry," Zoe whispered. "Stress."

Lauren nodded in understanding.

"What's going on? Who's dead?" Judy's eyes widened.

"Gio." Amy slowly rose. "And the authorities are on their way."

"I think we should all go somewhere else." Lauren spoke.

"What about the café?" Amy suggested. "But should we leave him here—" she glanced down at Giovanni's body "–alone?"

"I think it's better than ruining the crime scene," Lauren said gently.

"Come on." Zoe hooked her arm through Amy's. "Lauren and I can make everyone a hot drink. Maybe a cup of tea or hot chocolate instead of coffee?"

"And we should put sugar in the tea," Lauren added. She'd read a while ago that sugar was good for shock.

"I'll help you," Casey volunteered.

They entered the café space.

"I'll turn the machine on for you." Amy fiddled with the espresso machine. "If you three can handle the drinks, I'll get the cups out for you."

"No problem." Lauren smiled at her sympathetically, then felt guilty for doing so. Amy's partner – romantic or otherwise – was dead. She didn't think anyone should be smiling right now.

The others were subdued as Lauren, Zoe, and Casey made hot chocolate for everyone. No one had asked for a cup of tea.

"I can't believe it." Judy shook her head. "How could it have happened? We were all here."

"He said he had to make a phone call." Amy wrapped her hands around her cup, as if hugging it for warmth.

Frank checked his stainless-steel watch. "When are the paramedics arriving? Or will it just be the police? Good thing I don't have to get up early in the morning for work."

Lauren glanced at Zoe. She hoped Annie would be okay home alone. She would probably scold them when they did return, whatever time that would be.

Just as they finished their hot chocolate, the atmosphere a little awkward, flashing lights from outside the large glass windows snagged their attention. The paramedics had arrived.

Amy rose and let them in. She led the way out of the café, and down the hall, talking to the two men in a subdued voice.

"The police will be here soon," Amy said as she returned to the café.

"Good." Frank fidgeted in his chair.

"I hope this isn't going to be all too much for you, honey." Judy looked at her daughter anxiously. "Maybe you shouldn't go to school tomorrow."

"I'll be fine, Mom." Casey shook off her mother's concern.

A few minutes later, another vehicle pulled up outside the café. A middle-aged man with wavy brown hair got out and entered the café.

"Where are the paramedics?" he asked the group.

Amy pointed toward the hallway.

"I'll speak with you all shortly. I'm Detective Medhurst." He strode towards the area where the paramedics stood quietly.

When Detective Medhurst returned to the café area, Lauren was glad to see him. Everyone still seemed to be in a state of shock.

"I'll ask all of you some questions and get your names and addresses," the detective said. "Who would like to go first?"

"Me." Frank rose. "Although I have no idea what happened."

"Come with me." The detective led him out to the hallway. Lauren could see the two of them speaking, the detective taking notes, but couldn't hear what they said. The detective had placed Frank with his back to the others, through the glass door, so if anyone in their group was a lipreader, they still wouldn't know what Frank was saying.

"Do you want to go next, Judy? With Casey?" Amy asked.

"I would appreciate that." Judy smiled wanly and looked at her watch, decorated with crystals. "My goodness, it's almost ten o'clock!"

"It is?" Zoe checked hers, and Lauren did the same. "I hope we'll be able to open on time tomorrow," she murmured to Lauren.

Lauren nodded, feeling guilty even thinking of something like that when a man had lost his life. Amy looked bereft as she spoke quietly to Judy.

Frank returned to their little group. "He says I can go home now. I'm sorry about Giovanni," he told Amy.

"Thank you," she replied.

He gave them a wave and walked out of the café. A minute later, Lauren heard the muffled sound of his car engine.

Judy and Casey got up and headed toward the detective standing in the hallway. A few seconds later, Judy returned. "He wants to speak to us individually," she said.

A short while later, Casey came back into the café space, and Judy went to talk to the detective.

"He said Casey and I can go home," Judy told them a couple of minutes later. Judy fussed over the teenager as they left the building.

"You go first," Zoe told Lauren.

"Are you sure?"

"Yep." Zoe nodded.

Lauren walked toward the detective as if she were on trial. She'd just been on a date with Mitch, for goodness' sake, and hadn't felt like that.

After giving him her name, address, and phone number, she told him the little she knew. They'd eaten cake at the end of class, then a few minutes later, Giovanni had told them class was over. She and Zoe had said goodbye to Frank and Casey, and had gone to their car.

"And that's when I realized we forgot to buy some coffee beans," she told the detective who was looking at her in a focused manner.

"So you came back?"

"Yes." She detailed how she and Zoe had found Giovanni's body and that she'd called 911.

"What's so special about these coffee beans?" the detective frowned. "You're not the first person who's told me about them tonight."

"Giovanni said they were amazing," Lauren replied. "But …" she hesitated.

"Go on."

"He seemed to forget about them at the end of class. When I realized in the car that we hadn't bought any, that's when I remembered that he hadn't mentioned them again. And I thought he would have."

"Why?"

"Because that was the kind of person he seemed to be," Lauren said awkwardly. "He made sure to tell us about them in the middle of class and urged us to buy some, but later on he didn't bring up the subject again. I just thought it was a bit odd."

"I see." The detective wrote something in his notepad.

Once Lauren was free to go, she hurried over to Zoe in the café area. "Your turn."

"How was it?" Zoe asked.

"Not bad." And it hadn't been.

Zoe looked relieved when she rejoined Lauren. "We can go home now."

"We should say goodbye to Amy."

"Definitely."

They caught Amy just as she was heading out to the hallway.

"We just wanted to say goodbye," Lauren told her.

"And to say we're sorry about Giovanni." Zoe shuffled her feet awkwardly.

"Thank you." Amy nodded. "And thank you for helping with – everything – after …"

"You're welcome," Lauren said softly.

They made their way to the car, Zoe hopping in and buckling up.

"I'm glad that's over." She blew out a breath. "I feel awful about Giovanni – and Amy, but—"

"I know exactly how you feel." Lauren started the ignition. All she wanted to do was have a quick shower and slip into bed – with Annie. Hearing her soothing purrs and stroking her silky fur would make everything better – she hoped.

CHAPTER 8

Lauren and Zoe managed to open the cafe on time the next day – just.

"I was going to list my coffee cozy online today." Zoe looked disappointed. "But after what happened last night—"

"You should," Lauren told her.

"Brrt."

"I don't think anyone would think it was disrespectful."

"I'll do it tonight." Zoe smiled. "Do you want to help me, Annie?"

"Brrt!" Annie stood at the counter and looked up at Lauren and Zoe, her green eyes bright and intelligent. They'd just unlocked the door and so far there weren't any customers.

When they'd arrived home last night, Annie had seemed pleased to see them, and hadn't scolded them with little grumbles about staying out too late. Lauren had briefly told her what had happened, but stressed that the incident had occurred in a big city, and not in their café next door, or in Gold Leaf Valley.

The aroma of Ed's pastries wafted from the kitchen, making Lauren feel guilty she'd only baked two varieties of cupcakes that morning, instead of the usual three. But one of them was Norwegian Apple. They'd run out of almonds, so she'd put a walnut on top of the vanilla frosting, and tiny apple slices in the batter. She didn't know how authentically Nordic her cupcakes were with that sweet addition, but she knew her customers enjoyed a generous swirl of frosting.

"Hello." A dapper man in his sixties entered the café.

"Brrt!" *Hello!* Annie trotted to the *Please Wait to be Seated* sign, and looked up at him inquiringly.

"Hello, Liebchen." He bent a little stiffly to greet the cat. "Where shall I sit today?"

"Brrt." Annie sauntered slowly to a table in the middle of the room.

"Hi, Hans," Lauren called out.

"Hello, Lauren. And Zoe." He smiled at them. "How is everything today?"

"Good." Zoe sounded super cheery.

"Ah. Is something wrong?" he asked as he sat down at the table Annie had chosen for him.

"Maybe we shouldn't talk about it," Lauren warned her cousin as they approached Hans – and Annie. The cat jumped into the matching wooden chair and faced one of her favorites across the table.

"There's been a murder," Zoe burst out.

"Murder?" Hans paled.

"In Sacramento," Lauren added hastily.

"Oh." Hans looked relieved.

"It was at latte art class last night," Zoe informed him.

They quickly told Hans what had transpired the previous evening.

"Ach." Hans shook his head. "That is not *gut*. Not good at all. Hopefully the police will catch this killer quickly."

"Let's hope so." Zoe vigorously nodded.

"Brrt," Annie's tone was subdued.

"What can we get you, Hans?" Lauren asked.

"How about a latte?" Zoe chimed in. "I can try making a peacock design."

"I would love that." Hans chuckled. "What sort of cakes do you have today?"

"We have a new one," Lauren told him. "Norwegian Apple cupcake."

"With a walnut on top," Zoe added.

"I must try that," Hans said.

"We won't be long." Lauren and Zoe left him to chat with Annie.

"I hope today is going to be busy," Zoe said as they set to work behind the counter. "Then I won't have a flashback to finding Giovanni's body and the way he looked—" she shuddered.

Lauren had been trying to avoid thinking about it most of the morning.

"I know," she said sympathetically.

They were silent for a moment. Then the sound of the grinder brought them back to the task at hand.

"I'll make the latte," Zoe volunteered.

"Go for it." Lauren placed a cupcake on a white plate. "I'll take this over to Hans."

Since the senior was their only customer, she hoped business would pick up. She'd woken in the middle of the night, the image of Giovanni's dead, staring eyes jolting her awake. She needed something to distract her from thinking of that nightmare – and the terrible event of last night.

"It looks very interesting," Hans said when she placed the cupcake in front of him.

"Brrt," Annie said approvingly, peering over the table at the cake.

"I don't think it would be good for you if you had any," Lauren told her.

"Brrp." Annie gave a little grumble and settled down in her chair.

"Look!" Zoe carefully carried the latte over to the table. "A peacock." She presented the beverage to Hans.

"Ach, yes, I can see." Hans stared at the creation. "That is very clever."

"Brrt?" Annie asked.

Zoe carefully slid the coffee cup over to Annie.

"See? It's a peacock," Zoe said proudly.

"Brrt!" Annie seemed to approve of the pattern.

"Perhaps we should let Hans enjoy drinking it," Lauren said hastily, bringing the cup back to one of their favorite customers. "Sorry about that, Hans."

"No problem, as you say." Hans smiled. "It is good for the little one to see what you are doing."

They left Hans and Annie to enjoy their conversation.

"I'll check on Ed's pastries." Lauren hurried into the kitchen.

"They're ready," Ed grunted, his big burly arms pounding a mound of dough.

On the cooling rack was a tray of glistening apricot Danishes.

"They look and smell amazing." Lauren knew she had to save one each for her and Zoe. "I left out a new cupcake for you to try," she told him, seeing that it was still out on the counter.

"Thanks." He smiled briefly. "I'll have it during my break." The dough made a *thwap* sound on the counter.

Lauren picked up the pastries and headed back to the café space.

"Lauren, Mitch is here," Zoe sing-songed.

A million butterflies fluttered in her stomach and she stopped in her tracks.

She peeked over the tray of pastries.

"Hi." He smiled at her. He looked as good as ever in navy slacks and a dove gray dress shirt.

"Hi." The image of what might have been an almost kiss flashed through her mind.

"Let me grab these." Zoe took the tray from her unresisting hands.

"Is there somewhere we can talk?" Mitch asked.

"Yes. Why?" She looked around the still empty room, apart from Hans and Annie at a two-seater table. "In here? Or outside?"

"Here is okay." He headed to a semi-secluded table at the rear.

Lauren followed him, wondering what was wrong. Was he going to tell her he didn't want to go on another date with her? Somehow, she didn't think he was here for a swan latte.

He waited for her to sit down, then he did the same.

"I heard about last night. The murder at the café in Sacramento. That's where you were taking latte art class, right?"

"Right." She nodded.

"Are you okay?" He looked at her intently, as if trying to discover the answer for himself.

"I'm fine. We're fine. Zoe and me." Lauren hoped she wasn't babbling.

"Good. That's good." He nodded. "And you and Zoe made statements to the police?"

"Yes. How did you find out?" Lauren crinkled her brow.

"I heard about it this morning at work. I was going to stop by anyway, for a swan latte. I wanted to check you were okay."

"I am." She was now.

"And ..." he hesitated. "I think you should stay out of this one. I don't want anything to happen to you."

"It happened over an hour away," she told him. "Zoe and I are busy running this café. We only met the other people in the class for the first time last week. We have no intention of getting involved."

***

"So what did you say?" Zoe asked after work that day. This was the first

120

chance Lauren had had to tell her cousin about her conversation with Mitch.

"That of course we have no intention of getting involved in solving Giovanni's murder." She'd made Mitch a latte after that, even creating a swan on the surface of the crema, and they'd chatted for a few more minutes. But he hadn't brought up the topic of another date.

"Brrp?"

"Yes, really," she told Annie. "We don't know any of those people. I think we should let the police department handle everything."

"Yeah – I think you're right this time." Zoe shook off what might have been a disturbing image.

They finished stacking the chairs in silence. Lauren had already locked the front door and now Annie walked around the corners of the room as if checking nobody had dropped an important item without realizing.

"I think we should talk about more pleasant things," Lauren suggested as they trooped down the private hallway to the cottage. "Like you listing your crochet cozy online."

"Yes!" Zoe skipped into the cottage kitchen. "I'd nearly forgotten about it, with all the customers we had."

After Mitch had left, they'd been busy for the rest of the day. The Norwegian apple cupcakes had been a hit, along with everything else.

"I'm going to do it right now."

"Okay." Lauren put down the two apricot Danishes on the kitchen counter and opened a tin of meat in gravy. "Dinner, Annie."

Annie sniffed the bowl, then started licking at the gravy.

"I'm on the handmade craft site!" Zoe hurried into the kitchen with the laptop a short time later. "Look!"

Zoe's purple coffee cozy appeared on the screen. The fancy ruby and gold button looked good on it.

"You did it." Lauren smiled at her cousin.

"I don't want to say that until I actually sell it. I listed it at $9.99."

"You should show Mrs. Finch your listing at crochet and knitting club," Lauren suggested. "I'm sure she'd love to see it on there."

"Good idea." Zoe put the laptop on the kitchen table. "I'm going to see if I sell my cozy during dinner."

They enjoyed pasta with mushroom sauce, and the apricot Danishes for dessert. After practically every mouthful, Zoe refreshed the laptop screen.

"Maybe we should have a no devices rule during meals," Lauren teased.

"I thought it might have sold by now." Zoe sounded a little downhearted.

"It's only been up there for the last hour," Lauren replied. "You need to give people a chance to find it. Maybe everyone goes online shopping after dinner."

"Good point." Zoe cheered up. "I won't look at it for a while."

'A while' lasted a whole thirty minutes.

"No one's bought it." Zoe peered at the screen. "This one's sold. And this one." She pointed them out. They looked professionally crocheted and cute, but Lauren had to admit they didn't have the wow factor of Zoe's button.

"This one sold for much more than mine." Zoe squinted at the website. "Do you think I set my price too low?"

"I have no idea," Lauren said truthfully.

"Maybe I did." Zoe tapped her fingers on the kitchen table. "Huh. Maybe I should raise my price. But what if nobody buys it?"

"Why don't you keep your price the way it is for now?" Lauren suggested. At least Zoe's crochet cozy drama was taking her mind off Giovanni's death.

"Okay." Zoe chewed her lip, as if wondering that might be the wrong decision. "But – yeah – okay, yes, I will."

Lauren felt like hiding the laptop for the rest of the night. Instead, she suggested they watch something on TV. "But not anything violent."

"No." Zoe shook her head. "Something fun."

The three of them ended up watching a rom-com. Zoe grabbed the laptop as the end credits rolled.

"I'll just check before I go to bed." She clacked away on the keyboard. "I sold it!"

CHAPTER 9

"So, are you going to make another coffee cozy?" Lauren asked the next morning as they did a last-minute check before opening the café. Zoe had been in a good mood for the rest of last night.

"No." Zoe sounded glum. "I forgot to factor in the postage." She slapped her temple. "What a dummy I am. I woke up early this morning, all excited, and wrote down my profit – and after the yarn, the button, the listing fee, and now the postage, I'm lucky if I make any money at all on it."

"I'm sorry," Lauren said.

"Brrt." Annie looked sympathetically at Zoe.

"I got carried away with the button." Zoe groaned. "It cost three dollars. And it took me over one hour to crochet it, plus time sewing on the button."

"Are you going to post it to the buyer today?" Lauren asked.

"During my lunch break." Zoe cheered slightly. "I hope they enjoy using it."

"I'm sure they will," Lauren replied.

"Brrt!"

"Thanks, guys." Zoe smiled at them.

By the time it was noon, Lauren was ready for her own lunch break, but she shooed Zoe away.

"I'll take a break when you come back," she told her cousin.

"Thanks." Zoe grinned as she scanned the room.

"I'll be fine." They were half full, but all their customers had been served. And Ed was in the kitchen. Lauren knew he'd help out here if she was desperate.

"Okay." Zoe zipped out of the café, clutching a bag that contained her crocheted cozy.

"Only you and me, Annie." Lauren spoke to the cat. Annie had jumped down from her bed and had ambled to the counter, curious as to what Lauren and Zoe had been talking about.

"Brrp." *We can handle it.*

"Oh, look." Lauren's attention was snagged by a newcomer. "Judy. She was at latte art class on Monday night."

"Brrt." Annie trotted to the *Please Wait to be Seated* sign.

"Hi, Judy." Lauren waved to the older woman and came around the counter. "What are you doing here?"

"Oh, is this Annie?" Judy bent down. "She is just precious!"

"Brrt!" Annie seemed to agree.

"Annie will show you to a table if you like," Lauren told her.

"I can't wait to see that." Judy beamed.

"Brrt," Annie said importantly, leading the way to a table at the rear.

"Thank you, Annie." Judy sat down at the two-seater.

"Brrp." Annie hopped up on the opposite chair and studied the woman.

"I wish I could have a cat just like you," Judy told her in a soft voice. "Yes, I do."

"What can I get you?" Lauren asked, curious as to why Judy had stopped by.

"Oh, I don't know." Judy appeared to be perplexed by the question. "I came here because—" she looked around the room as if checking for eavesdroppers, and then lowered her voice anyway, "—I can't stop thinking about Giovanni. Wasn't it awful?"

"It certainly was," Lauren replied, hoping the image of Giovanni's dead, staring face wouldn't rise up in front of her again.

"And you and Zoe found him!"

"Yes."

"I thought – I don't know what I thought," Judy admitted. "That it might be easier to talk about it with someone who was there."

"That's certainly understandable," Lauren replied, wishing there was a spare chair at the table. She dragged one over from a vacant table and sank down.

"Brrp?" Annie asked softly, her green eyes looking concerned.

"I'm fine." She smiled at the cat. "It's good to sit down sometimes."

"You girls must be rushed off your feet all day." Judy scanned the customers eating and drinking. "Where's Zoe? I thought she worked with you."

"She's on her lunch break," Lauren said.

"So you're looking after all these customers yourself? That's impressive." Judy glanced at her approvingly.

"Thanks," Lauren replied. "But they all received their orders before Zoe left."

"So you have time to chat for a few minutes?" Judy asked hopefully.

"Sure." Lauren smiled. She liked the older woman, but she hoped Judy didn't want to talk about Giovanni.

"So, how are you and Zoe getting along with your latte art?" Judy asked. "I'm still stuck on a heart although I practiced a lot yesterday. I thought it would take my mind off things, you know?"

"I do." Lauren nodded. "Why don't I make you a coffee? I can try a peacock for your design."

"Oh, that would be wonderful." Judy beamed. "Casey has been practicing ever since class ended." She became somber. "She used to be such a happy child, so sunny-natured. Then—" she shuddered a little, "—the teen years hit. I think it must be all those hormones roaming around inside her. She just changed. Now all I get are one-word answers and sometimes a grunt. I thought going to latte art class would bring us closer together. Casey only seems happy these days when she's working at the café or doing her latte designs."

"I'm sorry," Lauren replied, not sure what else to say. She wasn't a mother – except to Annie.

"Brrt," Annie said softly, as if sympathizing with Judy.

"Oh, well." Judy sighed. "At least Casey has found something that's interested her. Ever since Monday she's spoken of nothing else except her plan to enter barista competitions. Perhaps it's her way of blocking out Giovanni's death." She lowered her voice.

"Miss me?" Zoe suddenly appeared at the small table. "Hi, Judy."

"Are you back already?" Lauren checked her watch. Surely she hadn't been sitting here that long?

"I thought you might need help." Zoe scanned the room, then focused on Judy.

"I thought I'd come by and visit your café," Judy said. "Annie is just darling."

"Isn't she?" Zoe grinned.

"I wish I could have a cat, but my husband's allergic."

Lauren remembered Judy remarking on that at latte art class.

"Have you tried our goodies?" Zoe asked.

"Not yet. You girls will have to tell me what I should get."

"Everything." Zoe giggled.

"You should try one of Ed's pastries," Lauren said.

"And one of Lauren's cupcakes."

"I promised I'd make you a peacock." Lauren rose.

"Can I get a cupcake to go for Casey?" Judy asked.

"Of course. We have Norwegian apple, triple chocolate, or orange poppy seed today." Judy finally settled on a triple chocolate for Casey, an orange poppy seed cupcake and an apricot Danish for herself, and a large mocha.

Lauren concentrated on creating the pattern on the surface of the coffee as Zoe plated the baked goods, and took care of Casey's cupcake.

"It looks great." Zoe peered over her shoulder as Lauren finished the pull through. "I bet you'd beat Casey in a competition."

"You think?" Lauren remembered how dedicated the teen had seemed at class.

"Definitely. Casey might have youth, but you've got experience."

"Hey! I'm only twenty-six." Lauren shook her head at her cousin's teasing.

They carried Judy's order to the table. Annie still sat with her.

"This looks wonderful." Judy admired the orange poppy seed cupcake, decorated with a swirl of orange frosting dotted with poppy seeds, and the glistening apricot Danish. "And the design—" she stared at the peacock on the surface of her mocha. "Casey kept telling me how good you were, Lauren, and now I can see what she meant."

"Thanks," Lauren replied, pleased at the compliment. "Casey is great at latte art."

"At least she seems to know what she wants to do with her life – for now, anyway." Judy took a sip of her coffee, her eyes widening in appreciation. "Oh, I do love this, girls. In fact," her voice became hushed, "I think it's better than the coffee Casey's café serves. But don't tell her that."

"We won't." Zoe mimed zipping her lips.

They left Judy to enjoy her order.

"Did Judy come all the way here just to check us out?" Zoe asked once they were behind the counter.

"No. I think she's feeling a little post-traumatic about Giovanni," Lauren murmured.

"Did she talk about him?" Zoe furrowed her brow.

"Not really."

"Maybe she just used him as an excuse so she could visit us," Zoe continued.

"Because she was curious?"

"Exactly. And don't forget, she said she loves cats but can't have one. Maybe she wanted to check out Annie as well."

"She's certainly doing that." Lauren glanced over at Judy's table. Annie continued to sit with her.

"I can look after things if you want to take your break," Zoe urged.

"Did you post your coffee cozy?"

"Yeah." Zoe's voice became glum. "And with the postage, I think I actually made a loss."

"Oh, Zoe." Lauren patted her cousin's shoulder.

"I'll be fine." Zoe straightened her spine. "You get some lunch and I'll look after things here."

"Okay." Lauren grabbed a panini from the case and hurried to the private hallway. She'd just take twenty minutes and then return to the café.

Once inside the cottage, Lauren sat down at the kitchen table and wiggled her toes. The one drawback to working in a café was the amount of time spent on her feet. Even wearing comfy shoes, the standing sometimes took a toll.

After she finished her quick lunch, she re-entered the coffee shop. Annie still sat with Judy.

"She's still here," Zoe whispered to Lauren. "I'll go over and see if she wants something else."

Lauren scanned the room, but the other customers seemed happy eating their lunch or chatting with their companions. A soft hum of conversation filled the space.

The entrance door opened. Lauren turned to greet the new customer, dressed in an amber skirt and short sleeved cream blouse.

Ms. Tobin.

She inwardly groaned. Then she remembered that their fussiest customer had actually mellowed last time she was here.

"Hi, Ms. Tobin." Lauren approached the tall, thin woman, who stood at the *Please Wait to be Seated* sign.

"Where's Annie?" Ms. Tobin frowned. "She always greets me."

"She's with another customer at the moment," Lauren informed her. "But I'm sure she'll come over when she knows you're here."

Annie treated Ms. Tobin as any other customer, always leading her to a table. But the feline somehow sensed that Ms. Tobin usually didn't care for any further interaction.

Perhaps Annie greeting her was the highlight of Ms. Tobin's day? As far as Lauren knew, the older woman did not have any pets.

As if Annie knew they were talking about her, she turned around in her chair, her silver-gray ears pricked. She jumped down and trotted over to the *Please Wait to be Seated* sign.

"Brrp?"

"I think Ms. Tobin would like a table, Annie." Lauren smiled at the cat.

"Brrt." Annie sauntered to a small table in the middle of the room.

"Thank you, Annie," Ms. Tobin told the cat as she sat down. She pulled out a tablet from her large leather handbag, and waved Lauren over.

"I'll have one of Ed's pastries and a large latte." Ms. Tobin barely looked at Lauren, instead focusing her gaze on the glowing screen.

Lauren waited for the woman to instruct her on how to make the coffee, but to her surprise, Ms. Tobin seemed lost in whatever she was reading on her device.

"Okay." Lauren wrote down the order and then departed. Annie accompanied her back to the counter.

"Brrp?"

"Would you like to take a break?"

Sometimes Annie seemed to enjoy being in the café all day, and sometimes she liked taking a break.

"Brrt!"

"Okay. Come on."

They passed Zoe sitting in Annie's chair opposite Judy, talking a mile a minute. Luckily, no customers were trying to attract her attention.

Lauren unlocked the door to the private hallway, and Annie scampered down the corridor. Once they were in the cottage kitchen, Lauren gave Annie a bowl of beef in gravy.

"See you after work." She smiled as Annie's plumy tail waved in the air as she investigated her lunch.

"Sorry." Zoe left Judy's table as Lauren returned to the café. "I know I shouldn't have sat down and started chatting but—"

"It's okay." Lauren waved away her cousin's apology. "I need to make Ms.

Tobin a latte." She showed Zoe the rest of the order.

"I'll do it." Zoe plated the apricot Danish. "Oh, it's the last one."

"So what were you talking about?" Lauren asked curiously as the espresso machine hissed.

"Judy was telling me about Casey. Her surly moods, and what a great barista she is."

"She told me the same kind of thing." Lauren concentrated on fanning the peacock's tail on the surface of the latte. She hoped Ms. Tobin wouldn't find fault with the pattern.

"Maybe Judy doesn't have a lot of people to talk to," Zoe mused.

"Maybe," Lauren said absently. "I'd better take this over to Ms. Tobin."

"Good luck!"

"Here's your order, Ms. Tobin." Lauren gently set the two items on the table.

Ms. Tobin barely looked up from her device.

"Thank you, dear."

Lauren's eyebrows raised slightly. Ms. Tobin had never called her *that* before.

"You're welcome," Lauren murmured, hurrying back to the counter.

"Well?" Zoe asked. "Did she complain about something?"

"No." Lauren shook her head.

"Huh." Zoe stared over at their prickliest customer. "What do you think she's doing on that thing?"

"Maybe she's absorbed in a new hobby," Lauren said.

"Ooh, I know. Maybe she's internet dating!"

Lauren stared at her. "You think?"

"Why not?" Zoe shrugged. "Even older ladies are interested in meeting men online these days. I saw some of their profiles on the site I used."

"I hope she's staying safe." Lauren frowned as she looked over at the older woman. Ms. Tobin's gaze was locked on her tablet screen as she tapped away on the device.

"Maybe her new romance is putting her in a good mood." Zoe grinned. "Her wardrobe seems to be lighter in color – she's not wearing that awful brown shade today."

Judy walked up to the counter, looking around the room as she did so.

"Where did Annie go?"

"She's taking a lunch break," Lauren replied.

"I'll definitely come by again." Judy pulled out a pink wallet. "You must get a lot of repeat customers for your coffee and cakes – and Annie, of course."

"We do," Zoe said cheerfully. She rang up Judy's bill.

"Come back anytime." Lauren smiled.

"We must have a get together." Judy dropped her change into the tip jar on the counter. "Everyone who was at latte art class."

"You think?" Zoe asked.

"Of course. It's nice spending time with people who've shared an experience with you. I mean, I love my friends at tennis club but their eyes start to glaze over when I talk about making a heart pattern with my milk. I tried to tell them about it last week." Judy gave a little sigh. "But you girls know exactly what I'm talking about."

"Yes, we definitely do." Zoe nodded.

"We're closed Saturday afternoon, Sunday and Monday," Lauren replied. "But Casey has school, doesn't she?"

"I don't know if Casey would be interested," Judy admitted. "But I'm sure Frank would be. And we could ask Amy."

"Give us a date and time and we'll see if we can make it," Zoe said.

They waved goodbye to Judy.

"I'm not sure if I really want to meet up with them," Lauren murmured to her cousin. "Does that make me a bad person?"

"Of course not," Zoe replied. "But it might be fun. We could show off with our designs and tell them where they're going wrong with theirs."

"If they're going wrong by then," Lauren said. "I like Judy. And Amy seems nice. Frank is okay."

"It would be something a little different. And sometimes different is good. It gets us out of a rut."

"That's true." Lauren thought back to their day out at a local casino. She'd had fun, and she'd won at Bingo. That had certainly been different. "Okay. If we're not working, we'll accept Judy's invitation."

"Deal."

The afternoon sped by. Lauren realized with a start that it was five o'clock. Their last customer had just departed.

"I'll lock up." Zoe bolted the entrance door.

Lauren's phone pinged. She read the text message.

"What is it?" Zoe appeared at her shoulder.

Lauren showed her cousin the screen.

"Judy wants to have a get together tomorrow at six p.m." Zoe frowned. "We won't be there in time."

"I'll let her know." Lauren didn't know whether she was relieved or not to have an excuse. Judy was certainly quick in organizing a class reunion.

"Isn't The Roasted Hipster in Sacramento where Casey works?" Zoe's nose scrunched. "I wonder if Casey's working a shift then? It might be fun if she made our coffees – we can see how good she really is."

"True," Lauren replied slowly. "But unless we can close a little early, Judy will have to start without us."

Zoe grabbed the phone and started typing.

"What are you doing?"

"Telling her six-thirty would be better for us." Zoe didn't bat an eyelash as she concluded her text message.

Lauren shook her head at her cousin's antics.

A few seconds later, a ping sounded.

"She said that's fine." Zoe waved the phone in the air.

"I'm glad that's settled," Lauren said drily.

CHAPTER 10

The next evening, Lauren and Zoe arrived at The Roasted Hipster, exactly on time.

"I can't believe we parked right outside." Zoe grinned as they approached the entrance. Blond wood accented with black decorated the storefront.

"Me neither." Lauren and Zoe had sped around the café, tidying it quickly and settling Annie into the cottage. She'd watched their antics with wide eyes, as if the two girls were creating an entertaining diversion for her.

"This should be interesting." Zoe charged into the café.

Lauren blinked as she entered the dark interior. The lights were dim – was it a deliberate design choice or did some of the bulbs need replacing? She just hoped she didn't bump into anyone – or anything.

"Over here!" Judy waved to them. She wore a pink top and white slacks. Sitting next to her was Frank, dressed in a black short-sleeved shirt and lightweight trousers.

"I knew he'd be here," Zoe muttered out of the side of her mouth to Lauren.

"Uh-huh," Lauren murmured.

"Hi, guys." Zoe smiled at the duo. "Is Amy coming?"

"She said she'd make it," Frank replied. In front of him was an empty gray coffee cup. "I arrived a little early, so I got a latte. I've never been here before."

"How was it?" Zoe asked.

"Not bad." He grinned. "But it tasted different to yours. They must use different beans."

"Hopefully Casey will be able to make our order," Judy put in. She pointed to the long counter. "There she is."

Casey wiped spilled milk off the work surface. Her brunette hair was tied back in a ponytail, and she wore a uniform that consisted of an olive t-shirt and pants.

"I'm starving," Zoe announced. "What sort of food do they have here?"

"Cakes," Judy said eagerly. Then her face fell. "But not as good as yours."

"Why don't we try one?" Lauren's stomach began to rumble. She hoped no one could hear it. It had been a long time since lunch and they hadn't had time to grab a snack before they left home.

"Good idea."

"I'll tell Casey what we'd like." Judy rose.

They gave Judy their orders and watched her thread her way to the counter. The place was busy, with at least half the tables taken with chatting customers. Music including clashing symbols and strange sounds played in the background.

"I hope Amy makes it." Frank checked his watch. "I wanted to ask her some questions about my tulip."

"How's your blog coming along?" Lauren asked politely.

"I've chosen a domain name and organized web hosting," Frank replied. "I've already written an article about how to create a heart and taken a photo of one I did at home."

"That's great!" Zoe sounded enthusiastic.

"A few more articles and then I'll get the affiliate links and ads rolling." Frank rubbed his hands together. "And continue to write more articles about making coffee at home."

"I hope it's successful," Lauren replied.

"It should be," Frank said confidently.

Judy came back to their table. "Casey will bring everything over," she told them.

"Is she going to make our lattes?" Zoe asked.

"Yes." Judy smiled. "I'm so glad she likes working here. It's much better for her than being bored and turning to alcohol or drugs—" she lowered her voice "—like some of her class mates have done."

"Really?" Zoe's eyes widened.

"Unfortunately." Judy shook her head. "I heard it from one of the other mothers at tennis club."

A couple of minutes later, Casey trudged over to them with a full tray.

"Regular latte, regular latte, regular latte, regular latte." She pointed to the four cups. On the surface of each was a peacock.

"Your peacock is great," Lauren praised.

"Thanks." Casey gave a brief smile. "And here's your gluten free pear and ricotta cake, Lauren, and this is Zoe's hazelnut raspberry slice. Mom was telling me about your café – and your cat. It all sounds cool."

It seemed like high praise coming from the teen.

"It is," Zoe assured her. "You should visit us one day."

"Maybe."

"Sorry I'm late." Amy hurried over to them, out of breath. The redhead wore a turquoise sleeveless shift dress and white canvas shoes. "This is a great idea, Judy. Have you all ordered?"

Amy decided on a regular latte as well.

"I'm looking forward to tasting it," she told Casey with a smile.

The teen smiled back, then made her way back to the counter.

"I think you've got the magic touch with my daughter," Judy sounded wistful. "I wish I had that."

"I'm sure you will again – in time," Amy consoled. "The teen years can be trying."

"For everyone," Judy replied with feeling.

Lauren sipped her latte. She hated breaking up the pattern, but she was curious as to how it would taste. A slight nutty bitterness. Perhaps it would be better as a mocha.

"Not as good as ours," Zoe whispered to her.

Lauren nodded in agreement as she forked up a mouthful of pear and ricotta cake. It sounded healthy, but the texture was a little dry, even with the ricotta. She noticed Zoe close her eyes as she munched on a piece of hazelnut raspberry slice.

"This is a bit gritty but it's got a good flavor," Zoe whispered in her ear.

Judy and Frank told Amy how sorry they were about Giovanni.

"How's the police investigation coming along?" Frank asked as he stirred his latte.

"I don't know." Amy shrugged. "They haven't found the killer yet – or if they have, they haven't told me. They asked if anyone had a grudge against Giovanni, but I told them I wasn't aware of anything. Not even a disgruntled customer."

"Maybe it was a robbery gone wrong," Judy suggested. "I saw a vagrant lurking down the road when Casey and I arrived the first night."

"Maybe," Amy replied. "We're usually closed at that time – apart from when we hold classes in the evening. Giovanni and I—" her voice broke "—were planning a lot more classes. He was keen to explore pour over coffee as well as continuing with latte art."

"I see," Lauren murmured.

Casey arrived with Amy's coffee, an impressive peacock on the surface.

"Have you been practicing bleeding hearts?" she asked Lauren and Zoe.

Lauren stared at the girl, the image of Giovanni's stabbed, bloody chest as he lay on the ground flashing before her eyes.

The group froze for a second, Amy's cup halfway to her lips.

All eyes were on Casey.

"What?" the teen asked. She scanned their expressions. "Oh. Sorry. I didn't mean—" a pink tinge swept her pale cheeks.

"It's okay, honey." Judy patted her daughter's hand. "You didn't realize what it would sound like."

Amy took a sip of her drink, as if she needed to fortify herself.

"No harm done," Frank said.

Lauren and Zoe nodded.

"I'd better get back." Casey fled to the other side of the room.

"Oh, dear." Judy sighed. "I know she didn't say that on purpose. I'm sorry, Amy."

I'm sure she wasn't being malicious." Amy set her latte down gently on the table. "I just don't know what I'm going to do without … without Giovanni."

"Were you two just business partners?" Frank asked curiously. "Or was it more than that?"

"Frank!" Judy admonished him. "I don't think you should ask that."

"It's okay," Amy said wearily. "We've been business partners for a few years. But lately, things had taken a romantic turn. We were just finding our way, you know?"

"Uh-huh." Judy nodded.

"I'm sorry," Lauren said.

"Yes," Zoe added.

"And now with the café – I can't even think of what I need to do. Hire a manager, I suppose. The place keeps – kept – both of us busy. I can't handle it on my own."

"Do you have employees?" Lauren asked. She hadn't seen any staff other than Amy and Giovanni at the evening classes.

"Yes. A couple of full timers, and some part-timers. You know, it was funny." Amy sipped her latte. "Giovanni had been talking about hiring Casey – said she was a natural barista and he was keen to teach her everything she knew. He thought with the right training she could go all the way to the world championships."

"Wow," Zoe murmured.

"Casey didn't tell me that." Judy frowned.

"He hadn't spoken to Casey about it yet. It was just an idea at this stage."

"I wish he could have trained me," Frank said wistfully. He flexed his hands. "I bet I could have a chance at the championships – if I had the right training and put in the time." He turned to Amy. "Hey, how about it? You could teach me everything I need to know and enter me into competitions. I could even work for you part-time, and I can write about my progress on my coffee blog!"

"Oh – um—" Amy's lips parted. "That is certainly an idea, Frank. But right now—"

"It's okay," Frank replied after a moment when Amy didn't say anything else. "You've got a lot to deal with. But keep me in mind if you need extra staff, okay? I've bought an espresso machine and already my cappuccinos are better than the stuff from the café near my house. I won't be going there again for a caffeine fix." He chuckled.

There was a small silence as they finished their beverages.

"Are you going to hold more classes in the future?" Frank asked.

"I don't know." Amy shook her head. "The classes were Giovanni's idea. He wanted to share his talent with the world – or at least Sacramento, for now. He even had an idea of expanding the classes, going on the road with them during the quieter periods, and charging more for them, since he was a barista champion. I said we should see how these classes did first."

"I thought one hundred dollars each was expensive," Zoe whispered to Lauren. "He wanted to charge more than that?"

"The whole situation is just so sad." Judy patted Amy's shoulder. "Let me know if there's anything I can do – even if you just want to talk to someone who was there. I visited Lauren and Zoe yesterday because I felt I needed to be with people who understood what I'd experienced."

"Oh, yes, your cat café." Amy's expression lightened a tad.

"Annie, their Norwegian Forest Cat, is just darling," Judy enthused. "I'm in love with her already after just one visit."

"That cat showed me to a table," Frank jumped in. "Never seen anything like it before."

"Oh, I must visit when I have time," Amy said. "When are you open?"

Lauren told her.

"We even got a review from a food critic recently," Zoe enthused. "From two, actually. But the first one died and then his assistant took over and re-reviewed us. We're mentioned in his online column."

"Who was that?" Frank looked at them keenly.

"Todd Fane, and his assistant was Brandon."

"Oh, I read about that," Frank said. "He was murdered, wasn't he?"

"Yes." Zoe nodded so vigorously, Lauren wondered if her head would fall off. "And we helped solve the murder!"

"You didn't!" Judy stared at them, her eyes wide.

"Uh-huh." Satisfaction sounded in Zoe's voice.

"We shouldn't be talking about this." Lauren frowned at her cousin. "I don't think it's the right time—"

"But it's the perfect time." Judy leaned across the table. "You could solve Giovanni's murder!"

CHAPTER 11

"No." Lauren's lips tightened. She remembered Mitch's warning not to get mixed up in the investigation.

Besides, she didn't know if she wanted to get involved. And it didn't have anything to do with Mitch's caution or the fact that she was dating him – if she *was* dating him.

Two murders already this year were two too many. She didn't need a third.

"Yes, we could." Zoe's eyes sparkled. "Couldn't we, Lauren?"

"No."

"Did you two really solve the food critic's murder?" Frank asked skeptically. "I didn't see any mention of you in the newspaper."

Zoe proceeded to tell them exactly how they got involved. Lauren's face flamed at the slightly embellished tale.

"But isn't it dangerous to do something like that?" Amy furrowed her brow.

"Yes." Lauren nodded. "And that's why we're not getting involved this time." She shot Zoe a warning glance. "I'm sure the police will be able to catch the killer – without anyone else helping them."

Zoe grumbled something under her breath. Lauren didn't want to know what it was.

"Well, I think it's a shame," Judy declared. "I hope the killer doesn't get away with it."

"I'm sure the police will catch whoever did it," Amy said. "They have the murder weapon, after all."

"I sure hope they solve it." Frank nodded.

They chatted for a few more minutes about coffee – Frank telling them in detail about the beans he'd tried so far and hadn't been impressed with. Once everyone had finished their lattes, Amy looked at her watch.

"I should be going," she murmured. "I'm sorry I can't stay longer, but there's so much paperwork to do now Giovanni …" Tears appeared in her eyes.

"Of course," Judy replied. "Remember, call me if you ever need to talk."

"I will." Amy dabbed her eyes with a handkerchief. "It was nice catching up with everyone. Maybe you'll all drop by the café for a coffee one day."

They said goodbye to the others, then Lauren and Zoe made their excuses and headed toward the exit.

"Well, that was—" Zoe began.

"Hey, Lauren." Casey beckoned them toward an alcove near the entrance.

"Are you okay?" Lauren asked. The teen's complexion was still a little flushed.

"I'm fine." Casey looked around as if to make sure nobody overheard them. "I just wanted to ask you about … bleeding hearts. You didn't say if you've tried making that pattern or not. Giovanni kept saying how good you were—"

"That's funny," Zoe interrupted. "Because he kept telling us how good *you* were."

Casey giggled, her expression lightening, making her look like the happy, sunny girl her mother had described.

"No, I haven't had a chance," Lauren told her. "I've been practicing swans and peacocks."

"I've been trying to do bleeding hearts. But I can't get it right, even after I watch online videos."

"Maybe Amy will have more classes in the future," Lauren said.

"That would be great." Casey sounded enthusiastic. "As long as Frank isn't in them."

"You don't like him?" Zoe asked.

"He's okay." Casey shrugged. "I guess. I just don't like it when he watches me."

"Watches you?" Lauren stared at the girl. "Where does he watch you?"

"Here." Casey pointed to the counter, where a man-bunned and bearded barista was making espressos. "He came the day after the first class. I served him, and he watched me like a hawk while I made the coffee. I thought he was going to jump over the counter and take over!"

"I know the feeling." Zoe nodded.

"Maybe he just wants to know how to make a good latte," Lauren said. "He seems very keen to learn everything he can about coffee."

"Too keen," Zoe said.

"But I thought he said today he hadn't been here before?" Lauren raised her eyebrow as she glanced at Casey.

"He definitely has been." Casey glowered. "He came again a few days ago – but I was just finishing my shift so Darman—" she nodded to the hipster barista at the counter "—served him."

"That's strange," Zoe mused.

"Yeah." Casey nodded. "I don't like it when people watch me like that – it makes me feel weird, you know?"

"Yes." Lauren certainly did know.

"If you feel uncomfortable about a customer, talk to your manager about it," Zoe advised.

"That's good advice," Lauren confirmed.

"I will. Thanks." Casey shifted. "I'd better get back to work."

They waved goodbye to her as they left the café.

"That's a bit strange, Frank lying about visiting the café, isn't it?" Zoe asked they got into the car.

"Yes." Lauren turned on the ignition.

"If he visits us again, there's no way I'm going to let him behind the counter," Zoe said in determination.

"Me neither."

***

Zoe yawned the next morning as she unlocked the door of the coffee shop.

"I hope you'll be able to stay awake for knitting and crochet club tonight," Lauren teased.

Annie had already hopped up in her bed, although she looked at Lauren and Zoe with interest. She'd only grumbled at them a little when they'd arrived home last night. Now, her ears pricked up at the mention of the club.

"Me, too," Zoe said ruefully. "It took me a long time to go to sleep last night – I don't know whether it was the coffee at Casey's café, or the fact that I was thinking about Giovanni's murder."

"I know the feeling," Lauren replied. But in her case, it was wondering why she hadn't heard from Mitch, as well as puzzling over Frank's lie that he hadn't been to Casey's café before.

Was Mitch regretting their date? She hadn't seen him since he'd stopped by the café earlier in the week and she'd made him a swan latte.

"I don't know what I'm going to do at crochet club tonight." Zoe sighed as she slid behind the counter. "I've finished my scarf, and I've mailed the crochet cozy to the lucky buyer – very lucky, since it actually cost me money to make it."

"Maybe Mrs. Finch will have an idea," Lauren suggested.

"Brrt!" Annie seemed to agree.

"I think you two are right." Zoe brightened. "I'll ask her tonight."

Customers began to arrive, keeping Lauren, Annie, and Zoe busy for the next hour. Lauren had just sat down to catch her breath, when the entrance door slammed open.

She startled at the noise. Casey stood there, her gaze darting around the room. Her hair looked as if she hadn't brushed it that morning, and her t-shirt wasn't tucked into her shorts properly.

"You have to help! Mom's going to be arrested!"

CHAPTER 12

"What?" Lauren hurried over to the teen.

"Brrt?" Annie trotted over to Casey.

"I heard them talking." Casey spoke so quickly, Lauren had trouble understanding her. "They're going to see if they've got enough evidence to get a warrant and arrest her!"

"Who's getting arrested?" Zoe zoomed up to them. "What are you talking about?"

"I think we should sit somewhere quiet first." Lauren gave Zoe a warning look.

The café was almost half full. Already, curious customers had craned their heads to see what the commotion was at the entrance.

"Brrt." Annie led the way to a four-seater table at the rear.

"It *is* true." Casey sounded distracted. "Your cat does show people to a table. I thought Mom might have made it up."

"Do you want something to drink?" Zoe asked as they all sat down. She studied the girl. "You look a little flushed."

"How did you get here?" Lauren crinkled her brow.

"I ditched school and drove here." Casey shrugged, as if missing school wasn't a big deal. "I didn't know who else to ask for help. Mom told me last night that you were going to investigate Giovanni's murder."

"We never agreed—"

"Tell us what happened," Zoe interrupted her cousin.

Casey drew in a deep breath and leaned toward them. "I was getting ready for school this morning when two cops showed up. They talked to Mom for a few minutes. Mom had sent me up to my room when they arrived, and when they left I watched them go. My window was open so I leaned out to try and overhear what they were saying. Then one of the guys' phone rang and I heard him tell his partner that they'd see if they could get a warrant to arrest Mom!"

"Wow," Zoe murmured, sitting back in her chair.

"Why would they arrest your mom?" Lauren asked.

"Because …" Casey hesitated. "Because when they were inside the house talking to Mom, I crept out of my room and down the hall so I could eavesdrop. They told Mom her fingerprints were on the knife!"

"How do they know that?" Zoe asked. "They didn't ask us for our fingerprints."

"Because Mom told me after they'd gone that she'd had a DUI a long time ago. She said it was a mistake – she'd only been over the limit by a tiny amount, but that's how they had her fingerprints on file."

"Amy brought in a cake toward the end of the second latte class," Lauren said slowly.

"That's right!" Zoe snapped her fingers.

"And Mom helped Amy tidy up everything afterward."

"I guess that's how your mother's fingerprints got on the knife," Lauren said.

"Yeah." Casey nodded. "That's what Mom told the cops this morning." Her shoulders slumped. "But I don't think they believed her. Because why else would they want to arrest her?"

"I don't know," Lauren said slowly. She had problems believing Judy could be the killer. But she couldn't imagine anyone in their class killing Giovanni.

"This is all my fault." Casey's brown eyes shone with wetness. "I knew I shouldn't have stolen those coffee beans, but I couldn't resist. And now Mom's going to jail!"

"What coffee beans?" Lauren asked.

"Brrt?" Annie stared at the teen.

"Beans from the café," Casey sniffled. "It wasn't that many – maybe three ounces. I just wanted to try them at home. See, I don't think they're using the right grind setting at the café, and that's why the coffee tastes a little bitter—"

"I was wondering about that last night," Zoe interrupted.

"So I thought I'd try making a latte at home with the same beans and experiment with the grind settings on my machine. And I was right – those beans definitely tasted better at home. So—" the enormity of the situation seemed to hit Casey once more "—that means Mom being in trouble is my fault. Because I'm a thief."

"I'm afraid I don't follow," Lauren admitted.

"Chaos theory," Casey explained. "You know, like how a butterfly flutters its wings in one country, which means an earthquake can happen in another country."

"Oh," Zoe said. "I get you."

"You have to help Mom," Casey pleaded.

"I don't think—" Lauren started.

"We will." Zoe nodded. "Definitely."

"We're not qualified—" Lauren tried to say.

"But Lauren's dating a police detective," Zoe put in. "If anyone can get the inside scoop, it's her."

"Zoe!"

"It's true," Zoe told her. "Okay, so you haven't seen Mitch since Tuesday, but I bet if you call him and tell him you've just baked a batch of vanilla cupcakes, he'll be here in the next hot second."

"Stop. Now." Lauren covered her face with her hands so nobody would see her flaming face.

"Brrp?" Annie placed a paw on Lauren's arm.

"It's okay," Lauren whispered, peeking through her fingers at Annie. "I'm hiding from Zoe."

"Brrt." *I understand.*

"And then," Zoe continued, as if Lauren's interruption hadn't happened, "You can grill Mitch about the murder and why they think Judy did it."

"Yes!" Casey sat up straight. "Do that!"

"But," Zoe looked at the teen, "you have to promise not to steal again. Even if it was for a coffee experiment."

"That's right," Lauren added. "And you need to pay back the café for the beans you stole—"

"Yes, put the money in the register when nobody's looking," Zoe suggested.

"Really?" Lauren frowned at her cousin.

"Okay." Zoe sighed. "You should do the right thing and confess to your boss, make restitution and beg not to be fired."

Casey wrinkled her nose. "But they'll terminate me for sure!"

"Maybe you could get a job at Amy's café," Lauren suggested. "She mentioned last night that she might need new staff soon."

"Amy really knows all about coffee." Casey looked interested. "Okay. I'll tell my boss about the beans if you promise to help Mom."

"Deal." Zoe grinned.

***

"Call him." Zoe shoved a cell phone into Lauren's hand.

Casey had left, promising to go to school for the rest of the day, as long as they kept their promise to help clear her mother's name.

"What if he doesn't want to talk to me?" Lauren stalled. She couldn't believe Zoe had volunteered them to snoop around in the investigation without talking over it with her first. Like adults.

She fixed a stern gaze on her cousin. "You're going to have to stop doing stuff like this, Zoe."

"I know." Zoe looked regretful. "I'm sorry. I got carried away. But I love when we sleuth and help solve the murder. And Casey looked so distraught, I wanted to help her."

"So did I," Lauren admitted. "But are we really right for this investigation? We don't know any of these people. It's not as if they're locals and they stop by the café every day."

"I guess we can call Casey and tell her we changed our minds." Zoe sighed. "But we'll have let her down. And then she mightn't come clean about stealing those coffee beans. What if she gets a taste for theft and goes down the wrong path and—"

"Fine." Lauren stabbed a couple of buttons on the phone. "But you are not to make decisions concerning both of us again unless you talk it over with me first."

"I promise." Zoe's voice sounded sincere. It seemed Lauren had gotten through to her. "I'm sorry."

"Okay." Lauren concentrated on listening to the line ring at the other end. Her stomach fluttered at the thought of talking to Mitch. Was she as bad as Zoe for doing this? Would he be annoyed that she only contacted him to ask for information on a murder investigation?

When Mitch answered the phone, Lauren forgot to speak for a couple of seconds. But with Zoe staring at her, practically willing her to ask him for inside information, Lauren hesitantly asked if she could talk to him about the investigation into Giovanni's murder.

"I'll be there in half an hour." His deep, masculine voice came through the cell phone connection.

"Well?" Zoe asked eagerly as Lauren ended the call.

Lauren chewed her lip. "I don't have any vanilla cupcakes."

"Is he coming over? What did he say?"

"He'll be here soon."

"Yes!" Zoe tap-danced behind the counter. "Oops. Mrs. Jones is waving at me. I'd better see if she needs anything." She hurried over to the middle-aged customer.

Lauren glanced over at Annie. She was curled up in her bed, seeming to have a snooze.

Lauren smoothed down her apricot t-shirt, neatly tucked into her pale blue capris, then surveyed the glass case containing her baked goods. Lemon drizzle, blueberry crumble, and triple chocolate.

It was okay for Zoe to be confident about Lauren asking Mitch for information. But she didn't know whether she was comfortable asking him questions about the investigation.

Maybe he wouldn't have *any* insider details. As far as she knew, the Sacramento police were working on the case.

She said goodbye to a few customers and greeted two more. Glancing at her watch, she noted that thirty minutes had passed already.

The next time the door opened, she looked over.

Mitch.

She caught her breath. Dressed in dark slacks and a smoke-gray shirt, he smiled at her as he strode toward the counter.

"Brrt." Annie hopped down from her bed and scampered over to him.

"Hi, Annie." He bent down to greet her.

"Hi," Lauren said.

"Hi."

Annie looked at first Mitch, and then Lauren. With a small "Brrp," she ambled back to her bed.

"What's up?" He looked at her with intent dark brown eyes.

"Would you like a latte?" she asked, trying to delay the moment.

"Sure." He nodded.

She busied herself making the coffee, wondering the best way to broach the subject.

"I'm glad you called," he told her.

"You are?"

"Yes. I've been meaning to stop in and see you, but I've been busy with work."

"Not Giovanni's murder?" Lauren paused foaming the milk.

"No, other stuff that's been happening."

"Has someone died in Gold Leaf Valley?" Lauren's eyes widened.

"No. Just a couple of burglaries, plus Elderblue Creek has asked for help – nothing too serious," he added.

"That's good." Lauren concentrated on pouring the milk into the cup, wiggling the jug until a peacock appeared on the surface of the crema.

"Wow." Mitch studied the design. "That's impressive."

"Thanks." She smiled. "Do you have time to sit for a few minutes?"

"Sure." He followed her to a small table toward the rear of the room.

She pretended not to notice Zoe winking at her while attending to a customer.

"So," Lauren drew in a breath once they were seated. "Judy's daughter came to see us today." She launched into the events of that morning. "Do you know anything about it?" she finished.

"No." He shook his head. "It's not my case. But …" he paused. "I do have some contacts in the Sacramento police department. I could put out some feelers—"

"That would be great." Lauren smiled. "Thank you."

"I might not find out much," he warned. "The detectives aren't likely to have enough to get a warrant, if Judy touched the knife when she was helping clean up. I don't think you should get involved."

"Zoe and I want to help Casey. You didn't see her – she was distraught over the possibility of her mom being arrested."

"You're a good person." He placed his hand over hers, making her pulse race. "I just don't want anything to happen to you."

"Me neither."

They chatted for a few more minutes, then Mitch asked her out for tomorrow night. Lauren didn't hesitate to say yes.

CHAPTER 13

"This is awesome," Zoe crowed. "You can grill Mitch again tomorrow night!"

"Zoe!" Lauren protested.

"And you won't miss crochet club tonight. How is your scarf coming along?"

"I haven't had time for much knitting this week," Lauren confessed. After Mitch had left, the rest of the day had become busier and she hadn't had a chance to fill Zoe in.

Now, after closing the café at five and tidying up, Lauren was ready to grab some dinner and get ready for knitting and crochet club. She didn't want to think about her impending date with Mitch, or it would occupy her whole mind. She'd let herself think about it tomorrow.

"Maybe you need to try something different," Zoe suggested over the drone of the vacuum as she ran it over the hardwood floor. "If I can't think of anything to crochet tonight, I might ask Mrs. Finch if she can teach me another craft."

"Like sewing?" Lauren teased.

"Not sewing." Zoe shuddered.

"Brrp!" Annie had been quiet until now, seemingly content to let Lauren and Zoe do all the talking. Now she loped toward them, batting something white and pink in front of her.

"What is it?" Lauren bent down to the cat.

Annie pushed the item towards Lauren's feet.

"It's a flower stuck on a paper napkin." Zoe turned off the vacuum and stared at the small item.

"Annie, do you have anything on your paws?" Lauren examined the cat's paws one by one, but they were spotless. Good. But just in case, she ran into the kitchen, grabbed a clean cloth, damped it, and gently wiped Annie's feet.

"Brrp." Annie gazed at her find.

"It looks like a pink fondant flower." Lauren reached to pick it up, then drew her hand back. "Maybe I should use gloves to handle it."

"Good idea."

Lauren hurried back to the kitchen and grabbed a pair of disposable gloves.

"Maybe a customer dropped it when they were eating their cupcake," Zoe suggested.

Lauren bent down and picked up the flower.

"I haven't decorated cupcakes with fondant for a while," Lauren admitted. "And I can't remember the last time I made pink flowers." She glanced at Zoe. "Please tell me this thing hasn't been on the floor for weeks – or months."

"No way." Zoe held up her hands. "I've been doing a good job of vacuuming …" her voice trailed off and a guilty look flashed across her face "… apart from this week. We've been busy, with the get together at Casey's café," she added defensively.

Lauren turned over the find in her gloved hands. It seemed like an ordinary fondant flower stuck to a napkin, the kind she sometimes made herself.

An image flashed through her mind.

"This looks like something that was on the cake at latte art class."

"You're right!" Zoe peered at the flower. "The cake that we all ate at the end of the second class. "It was delicious. Just about as good as your baking."

"So how did it end up here?" Lauren posed the question. "If it did come from that cake."

"Judy was here." Zoe tapped her cheek.

"And Frank – but was that before or after the second class?"

"And Casey," they both blurted at the same time.

Lauren and Zoe stared at each other.

"No way." Zoe shook her head.

"Is there a chance that we could have picked up the flower at latte class and somehow it got transferred to the floor in here? On a napkin?" Lauren hoped that wishful thought could be true.

"I don't see how." Zoe wrinkled her nose. "Unless it stuck to our shoes."

"Annie, where did you find this?" Zoe pointed to the flower in Lauren's outstretched hand.

"Brrp." *Over here.* Annie sauntered to the rear of the café, her nose in the corner as she sniffed, seeming to check that there wasn't anything else interesting waiting to be discovered.

There wasn't. The floor looked clean enough to eat on.

"Maybe another customer dropped it," Zoe suggested. "They could have decorated a cake at home."

"It's possible, I guess," Lauren sighed. "I'd better put this in the kitchen, just in case it's important."

"Somewhere safe," Zoe said.

"Yes."

Lauren carefully wrapped the find in plastic film, then in a plastic bag, adding a note on top that said *Do Not Touch.* She placed it in the refrigerator. It should be safe enough like that.

"Are you going to tell Mitch?" Zoe asked as she waited at the entrance to the private hallway to the cottage, Annie standing beside her.

"Definitely."

***

At crochet and knitting club that evening, they told Mrs. Finch about Giovanni's death, and finding the fondant flower.

"You're very clever, Annie," the elderly lady praised the cat. "It could be a clue."

"Brrt!" Annie said proudly.

Lauren continued knitting her scarf, while Zoe explained her craft dilemma to Mrs. Finch, as well as filling in the senior on selling her crocheted cozy.

"Perhaps you should try something new, Zoe."

"That's what I was thinking." Zoe sank back against the fawn sofa cushions in Mrs. Finch's living room. "Do you have any suggestions?"

"Well." Mrs. Finch closed her eyes for a moment. "I do remember my son making a string art picture at school. Of course, that was many years ago now."

"Huh." Zoe looked interested. "String art. What's that?"

"You hammer in some small nails on a canvas or a piece of wood, and then make a design using pretty colored string," Mrs. Finch informed her.

"Ooh." Zoe whipped out her phone from her small purse. "Let me see what I can find."

After a few seconds pressing the buttons on her phone, Zoe held out the screen to Lauren and Mrs. Finch. "Look! It's a sun."

A photo of a string art sun greeted them, using gold and orange thread for the sun's rays, mounted on a black background.

"I could totally do that," Zoe enthused. "You're awesome, Mrs. Finch!"

"I suppose this club will now be called the knitting, crochet, and string art club," Lauren teased. "And to think that two months ago it was just plain old knitting club."

"Brrt!"

***

By the time Saturday evening arrived, Lauren was a nervous wreck. She'd told Zoe she'd inform Mitch about finding the fondant flower, but all day she'd been second-guessing herself.

"I'd better tell him as soon as he gets here," she muttered to the mirror as she brushed her hair.

"Brrp?" Annie asked curiously as she sat on the bed, 'supervising' Lauren's preparations.

"Mitch might want to bag the fondant flower you found," she explained to the feline. "For evidence."

"Brrt," Annie sounded as if she agreed with the statement.

"He's here!" Zoe burst into Lauren's bedroom. "He's walking up to the porch."

By Zoe's behavior, anyone would have thought that a date visiting the house was a rare occurrence. Maybe it was for Lauren in the last couple of years, but until recently, Zoe had been interested in finding 'the right guy'.

"Thanks." Lauren put down her hair brush and picked up her purse.

"Annie and I will have fun on our own tonight." Zoe grinned at her. "Won't we?"

"Brrt!"

"Where are you going?" Zoe asked Lauren.

"To that new restaurant just outside town," Lauren told her. "The bistro."

"Ooh, yes." Zoe's eyes lit up. "We should go there one day. I'd love to know what it's like."

"I'll fill you in when I get home." Lauren smiled.

"Deal."

The doorbell rang.

Lauren hurried to the front door. All thoughts of the fondant flower fled her mind as she stared at Mitch. Dressed in what Lauren had come to think of as his typical outfit of dark slacks and this time, a navy dress shirt, his appearance took her breath away.

"Hi," There was warmth in his voice.

"Hi."

There was a pause as they gazed at each other for a long, silent second.

Fondant flower. Right.

Lauren's brain kicked in and she quickly told him about Annie's find the previous evening.

"Have you got it?" he asked.

"It's in the café kitchen."

"I'd better take a look at it."

He followed her through the cottage and into the private hallway that led to the coffee shop.

Lauren led the way into the commercial kitchen and opened the refrigerator.

Mitch carefully pulled out the plastic packet and peered at the cake decoration and napkin.

"I'll write you a receipt." He dug out a notebook from his shirt pocket.

"You have your notebook with you?" Lauren crinkled her brow.

"You never know when it comes in handy." He smiled. "Like right now." He scrawled a receipt and gave it to her. "I guess we'd better stop at the station on the way to the restaurant, so I can log this. You don't mind, do you?"

"No." She'd told him how she and Zoe thought it could be a possible clue, after all.

Mitch ushered her into his car, and drove to the Gold Leaf Valley police station. After assuring her he wouldn't be long, he strode inside the brick building.

Lauren checked her reflection in her tiny compact while she waited in his car. It was probably best they'd gotten the investigation business out of the way before they had dinner. Then they didn't have to talk about it.

But what *would* they talk about? Lauren's heart stopped beating for a second. What if Mitch thought she was the most boring person ever? Most of her life revolved around the café, Annie, and Zoe. Mitch had told her he'd never had much to do with cats until he'd met Annie. What if he thought she was a crazy cat lady?

Before anxiety made her chew her lip color off, Mitch came out of the building and entered the car.

"All set." He fastened his seatbelt. "I've locked it away for evidence and I've left a message for the Sacramento detectives."

"Thanks." She smiled.

During the drive to the restaurant on the outskirts of Gold Leaf Valley, she told him about Zoe's new enthusiasm for string art.

"How's your scarf coming along?" he asked.

He'd remembered. Warmth swept through her as she ruefully told him she didn't think she'd ever finish it.

"I'm sure you will," he assured her.

Lauren enjoyed a pork chop with four varieties of apples, while Mitch ordered the seared salmon. Over their meal in the dimly lit restaurant, he lightly touched on the investigation, telling her he'd update her with any news he received from the detectives involved, but once again reiterating he didn't think it was a good idea that she and Zoe got involved.

They moved on to more pleasant topics, such as Lauren enthusing about the hiking she and Zoe enjoyed sometimes on the weekend.

"Have you been to the Tahoe National Forest?" she asked, her spoon poised over her dessert of chocolate crème brulee.

"No, but I'd like to." His dark brown eyes crinkled at the corners as he gave her his full attention. "Maybe we could go together one day."

"Yes," she replied, her heart skipping a beat.

It was only when Mitch drove her home that Lauren wondered if Zoe and Annie were waiting up for her once more. She hoped they weren't going to spy on her through the window again.

As Mitch pulled up outside her house, she turned to him.

"Zoe and—"

"I had the same thought." He chuckled. "I'm glad they're looking out for you."

He walked her up the porch steps. The warm glow of the light provided a golden contrast to the navy twilight around them.

Lauren peeked through the window, partially covered by the drapes, but couldn't detect two inquisitive faces peeping out at her. Unless they were hiding.

"I can't see anyone," she told him as she turned to face him.

He was closer than she thought. A hint of light citrus teased her senses.

"I had a great time tonight." His voice was husky.

"So did I," she murmured.

"Let's do it again. Soon."

"Okay."

He cupped her face in his hands and kissed her.

Lauren melted, not even caring if her cousin and her cat were watching. As far as she was concerned, Mitch could kiss her all night long.

CHAPTER 14

Sadly, he didn't. After that long, tender kiss, he left, promising to call her next week.

Lauren floated into the house.

No Zoe and Annie.

She'd half expected them to pop out at her as soon as she closed the front door.

"I'm home," she called out.

"In here." Zoe's voice sounded from the living room.

Zoe and Annie were curled up together on the sofa, watching TV.

"How was it?" Zoe asked.

"Great." A soft smile played on Lauren's lips.

"Did you tell him about the clue Annie found?"

"Uh-huh."

"I wish someone would kiss me like that." Zoe clapped a hand to her mouth. "Oops!"

"You *were* spying!" Lauren shook her head.

Annie looked the picture of innocence, her green eyes wide, as if she were trying to bat them.

"Yep," Zoe cheerfully admitted. "Except this time we were going to pretend we hadn't, weren't we, Annie?"

"Brrt." *Yes.*

Lauren filled them in on her date, flopping down on the sofa next to Annie.

By the time she'd finished, she was struggling to contain a yawn.

"Ask Mitch if he has any hunky police friends." Zoe's suggestion sounded like an order. "Maybe we could double date one day!"

"I'll ask him," Lauren promised. Her cousin deserved to find a nice guy who suited her personality. Maybe Mitch did know someone.

"Then all we have to do is find a boyfriend for Annie and we'll be all set," Zoe concluded.

"Brrp?" Annie's eyes and mouth rounded in an O. She looked like she wasn't sure about *that* idea.

***

On Sunday, they visited Mrs. Finch, and then on Monday morning, Zoe declared she was going to Sacramento for the day. As long as she could borrow Lauren's car.

"You should come too," Zoe informed her.

"What are you going to do there?"

"String art shopping. I don't think the handmade shop here carries that sort of stuff. And," Zoe drew in a breath, "I thought I – we – could visit Amy's café."

"What for?" Lauren asked curiously.

"For a latte. And we could see how Amy's doing."

"Okay." Lauren didn't have anything planned for the day – she'd thought of coming up with some new cupcake ideas, but a day out did sound like fun. And it would be interesting to try Amy's coffee.

"I wonder if Judy's been arrested yet?" Zoe mused.

"I hope not." Lauren shivered. What would she do if she was ever arrested? She hoped she wouldn't fall apart.

Annie wandered into the kitchen to join them.

"Will you be okay if Zoe and I go shopping in Sacramento?" Lauren asked the cat.

"Brrt." *Yes.*

"We'll be home for dinner tonight." She shot Zoe a glance. "Won't we?"

"Of course," Zoe replied breezily. "There are only a couple of shops I want to go to – and Amy's café, of course. By then we might be hungry so we could have lunch somewhere, but after that, we'll probably come straight home."

"I'm glad you've got a plan," Lauren said drily.

She spooned some of Annie's food into a clean bowl.

"Here's your lunch," she told the feline. "And I'll make sure we're not home too late."

"Brrt." Annie sniffed the meaty mixture, gave it a lick, then wandered into the living room.

"Let's go." Zoe checked her watch. "I'm going to make an owl - no, a moon – no, a rose – no, a poppy." She waved her phone in the air. "There are so many different designs to choose from!"

Lauren grabbed her purse, said goodbye to Annie, and locked the cottage door behind her.

"It will be good to check up on Amy as well," Zoe told her as they fastened their seatbelts. "And her coffee."

A latte right now sounded perfect. Or perhaps a mocha. One she didn't have to make herself.

Lauren loved running her café and making the best coffee she could for her customers, but sometimes it was nice to be waited on for a change.

Just over one hour later, they arrived in Sacramento.

"We should visit Amy first," Zoe suggested. "I'm dying for a coffee, anyway." She winced as soon as her words left her mouth. "Sorry. Bad choice."

"It's okay." Lauren navigated the streets until they arrived at Amy's café. There was one parking spot left nearby, and she managed to parallel park.

"I'm hungry too," Zoe admitted. "Let's get something to eat here."

Lauren looked at her watch. It was eleven.

"Okay." It could be an early lunch.

Zoe pushed open the door.

About one quarter of the white wooden tables were taken. Otherwise, it all looked the same as it had during latte class – except today, there would be no Giovanni.

"Look, there's Amy." Zoe gestured to the slender redhead behind the counter.

"Hi." Zoe gave her a big smile as they walked up to the counter.

"What are you girls doing here?" Amy looked a little flustered.

"It's our day off," Zoe explained. "We thought a little retail therapy might do us good."

"Of course." Amy nodded. "What can I get you?"

After ordering a mocha and a slice of cake each, they chatted to Amy as she made the drinks.

"Are you here on your own?" Lauren asked.

"For the moment." Amy filled the portafilter with richly scented ground coffee. "Apart from—" she nodded toward the middle of the room "— Frank."

"He's here?" Zoe's eyes rounded.

"Yes. Says he wants to learn all he can about making espressos."

"You're going to allow him behind the counter?" Lauren asked, remembering that she and Zoe were reluctant to do so.

"No." Amy shook her head. "If he scalds or hurts himself, I don't want to be responsible. I told him he could watch from the customer side of the counter when it wasn't too busy."

"Did he?" Zoe's eyes were bright with interest.

"For a while." Amy steamed the milk, the hissing noise of the wand making a backdrop to their conversation. "And then he went over there to enjoy his macchiato."

"Hi, Lauren, and Zoe." Frank made his way toward them from a table in the center of the room. He wore gray slacks and a short-sleeved beige shirt. "I didn't expect to see you here."

"Shopping spree," Zoe replied airily. "We thought we'd drop by for a coffee and something to eat while we're in the city."

"You can't go past the espresso here." Frank beamed, gesturing to Amy. "It's the best."

"Really?" Lauren tilted her head. Better than hers and Zoe's? Now she really was curious to try Amy's coffee.

"Why don't I join you while you drink yours? My table is big enough for all of us." He motioned to a four-seater.

"It's ready, girls." Amy indicated two steaming cups. Each had a peacock design on the surface.

"They look great." Lauren smiled at the older woman.

"What did you get to eat?" Frank peered at the white china plates filled with a piece of cake that was an orange color, with flecks of carrot. "I haven't tried that. Amy, what's that called?"

"Carrot zucchini cake," Amy replied a touch wearily.

"Maybe not then," Frank replied. "I have to be careful with the vegetables I eat. Don't want too much gas." He chuckled.

Frank turned toward his table, and Lauren, Zoe, and Amy shared a glance of frustrated ruefulness.

"So, what have you two been up to?" Frank asked as they sat down at the table.

Lauren stirred her mocha, reluctantly breaking up the design while she fished for a reply.

"This and that," Zoe replied, then slurped her coffee. "Excuse me."

"The coffee's good, isn't it? Now, this is the sort of espresso I want to make at home. I'll have to ask Amy what kind of beans they use."

"It's not the beans Giovanni was selling on his last – that night?" Lauren wished she could take back the question.

"I don't think so." Frank shook his head. "I've tried those beans, and they are good, just as Giovanni described. But the coffee Amy made me this morning tasted different."

He launched into a detailed description of the differences he perceived between the two blends. Lauren glanced at her cousin – Zoe's eyes appeared to be glazed over.

Frank's droning voice allowed her mind to drift for a moment – as she enjoyed her carrot zucchini cake, and the rich chocolate coffee taste of her beverage. The mocha was just as good as Lauren's, and if she was honest with herself, maybe a *little* bit better. As she sipped, Casey's visit to their café flashed through her mind.

"Have you visited Casey's café?" Lauren asked when Frank paused for breath.

"Yes, on that day we all met up there," he replied.

"Not before then?" Lauren pressed.

Zoe's gaze cleared and she darted a glance between her cousin and Frank.

"I might have." Frank shrugged. "Is it important?"

"Casey told us you stopped by there before our class reunion," Lauren informed him.

"Did she?" he hedged.

"Uh-huh," Zoe confirmed.

"She said you were watching how she made your coffee," Lauren added.

"Did you think she was going to poison you?" Zoe asked.

"No!" Shock froze his face. "I was just …"

"What?" Lauren encouraged in a gentler tone.

"I was curious," he confessed. "I heard Giovanni raving about her barista skills in latte art class, so I thought I'd check out where she worked. I didn't know she would be working at the exact time I got there, but I guess I was hopeful." He sighed. "I just wanted to know if she was as good as Giovanni thought she was."

"And is she?" Zoe asked curiously.

"Yes. She's pretty good," he replied. "She's only a teen, remember. And she made a swan design on my latte."

"How did you like the coffee?" Lauren asked, remembering she hadn't liked it that much. "What did it taste like?"

"Not bad, but I thought it was a little bitter," he replied. "But she made it like a pro. Maybe the beans that café is purchasing aren't the best quality, or they're old. I couldn't fault Casey's technique."

"Why did you lie about it?" Lauren crinkled her brow.

Frank rubbed his neck. "Because I didn't want people to think it was weird. How could I say to Judy, 'Yes, I've been here before because I wanted to check out your daughter's barista skills?'"

"That makes sense. I guess," Zoe murmured.

"Everything okay?" Amy approached their table.

"Fine." Lauren summoned a smile. "That mocha was great."

"So was the cake," Zoe added. She turned to Lauren. "Maybe we should think about having vegetable cupcakes – with frosting, of course."

"Of course," Lauren replied drily.

"Do you have time to join us, Amy?" Zoe scooted closer to Lauren. "There's plenty of room."

"Maybe for a minute." Amy sat down next to Frank.

"Have you heard anything about Judy?" Zoe asked.

"No. Why?" Amy stared at them.

"Because – because—" Zoe turned to Lauren, seeking help.

"We're worried she might be arrested," Lauren blurted.

"Arrested? For Giovanni's murder?" Shock flickered across Frank's face.

Zoe launched into the story of Casey visiting their café, worried about her mom being arrested because she handled the cake knife.

"I certainly haven't heard anything," Amy said. "Judy has my phone number – surely she would have called if they did arrest her? Not from the police station, obviously. But when they let her go home? I handled the knife, too, and haven't heard anything lately from the detectives."

"Maybe the killer didn't wipe the handle completely," Zoe said. "He – or she – might have wiped off your prints, but not all of Judy's."

"I'm glad I didn't touch that knife." Frank chuckled.

The three women *looked* at him.

"Sorry." He held up his hands. "That was in poor taste."

"What are you going to do now, Amy? With the café?" Lauren asked delicately. "Are you still going to hire a manager?"

"I haven't done anything about employing a manager yet, but Casey is going to work for me," Amy replied.

"She is?" Lauren shared a secretive glance with Zoe.

"She came in on the weekend and said she'd love to work here and learn as much as she can from me."

"You're going to hire her?" Frank asked.

"Yes. After school and for a few hours on the weekends. Giovanni was right about her talent. She's going to train for the next barista competition that's held locally, and the café will sponsor her."

"But ..." Disappointment and frustration snuck across Frank's expression. "I thought you weren't going to take on another barista right now. I'd *kill* for the same chance Casey's getting. I asked you for a job first, remember?"

"Casey has experience," Amy replied awkwardly. "When you mentioned you'd like to work for me, I just wasn't in the right frame of mind to take on a trainee. My workload has practically doubled with Gio gone. I don't have time to teach a beginner. I'm sorry, Frank."

"You could ask around at all the cafés in the city," Zoe advised him. "Hey! If

Casey quit that café, maybe they're looking for a new barista there."

"If Amy won't hire me without experience, who will?" Frank shoved his chair back. "Why do people think being over fifty is too old to do anything? I don't *need* a job – I just want to learn all I can about the coffee biz. Is that too much to ask?" He strode through the room, knocking over a chair in his haste to leave.

"Wow," Zoe said softly.

"I know," Lauren murmured.

"This is my fault." Amy sank back in her chair and massaged her closed eyelids. "I shouldn't have brushed him off when he first asked me to train him. I didn't realize it was so important to him."

"You have a lot to do right now," Lauren told her. "It's totally understandable."

"We wouldn't let him make a coffee on the machine in our café," Zoe told her. "But I don't think that makes us horrible people."

"No." Lauren shook her head. "I don't think it does."

"Of course not." Amy opened her eyes and straightened her spine. "You two are right. Who I choose to employ is my business, not Frank's."

"Maybe he could start his own café," Zoe posed. "Or buy a franchise."

"He might like that idea." Lauren nodded. "If we see him again, we must remember to mention it to him."

There was a short silence.

"Which barista competitions did Giovanni enter?" Zoe asked curiously. She glanced at Lauren, before refocusing her attention on Amy. "I had some time this morning and did an online search for his name. But the competitions I found that he won were old, like eighteen and nineteen years ago."

"You didn't tell me you did that," Lauren commented.

"I was going to, but then I was busy persuading you to come with me today," Zoe replied. "Oh, and there must be at least one other person called Giovanni Voltozini because there were photos of another guy with the same name – he was good-looking, as well." She looked at Amy expectantly.

Amy flushed, then paled. "Oh, well, you know." She laughed uncertainly. "I'm sure Gio wasn't the only person in the world with that name – how many Zoe Crenshaws are out there?"

"I guess." Zoe frowned. "But what about the barista championships he won? Is there anything more recent?"

Lauren nodded in agreement as she watched Amy. The older woman fiddled with a sugar packet from the small bowl on the table.

The silence stretched. Around them, they could hear the other customers chatting to each other, and the occasional laugh or giggle.

Amy ripped open the packet. White grains of sweetness spilled onto the table.

"I'm no good at this." Despair filled her expression.

"No good at what?" Lauren's tone was low.

"At any of this." Amy waved a hand around the room, seeming to pause at a portrait of Giovanni on the wall. "You're right, Zoe." She slumped in her chair.

"Which part?" Zoe furrowed her brow.

"All of it." Amy passed a hand over her eyes. "If I tell you, do you promise not to tell anyone?" She hesitated. "Maybe I shouldn't even ask you that."

"We promise," Zoe said eagerly.

Lauren sighed inwardly. She didn't like keeping her word about something unless she knew exactly what it was.

Amy looked around, then leaned toward them. Nobody seemed interested in their conversation.

"Gio didn't win those competitions," she whispered.

"What?" Zoe's eyes widened. "But the class info said he was a world-renowned—"

"I know." Amy sighed. "I felt sick when I found out, but by then it was too late to do anything about it."

"What do you mean?" Lauren asked.

"When Gio and I went into business together opening this café, I truly believed he was who he said he was. I met him when we worked at another café on the other side of the city – he was the manager, and I was the assistant manager. We became tired of the substandard coffee the owner used, and he wouldn't let us buy better, fresher beans, either, because it would cost more. Eventually, we decided to open our own café, and have the best quality of everything."

"I'm with you so far." Zoe nodded.

"Me too," Lauren said.

"Our café opening was a success. Part of our advertising was promoting Gio's qualifications as a barista champion – he'd told me that he'd won plenty of competitions in Italy before coming to the U.S. Customers flocked here, wanting their latte made by a winner. But then …" Amy hesitated.

"But then?" Lauren encouraged.

"I was as curious as you, Zoe," Amy continued. "Things were starting to get romantic between me and Gio, so on my day off, like a lot of women nowadays, I typed his name into a search engine. I saw photos of another Giovanni Voltozini, and those barista competition results you found."

"What did you do?" Zoe asked.

"I asked Gio why those contests he'd entered were so long ago. He tried to brush it off, but for once I wouldn't let him control the conversation. I pressed him until he admitted that he hadn't entered those competitions – it had been his best friend in Italy."

"No way!" Zoe's mouth parted.

"Not only that, but he also confessed he'd never entered a barista competition. He claimed he was going to, because he worked in a café with his best friend, the real Gio, and he was qualified, but then the real Gio died in a motorcycle accident. He said he was so devastated he wanted to start a new life, and thought he would honor his friend by assuming his identity and moving to the U.S. He didn't think it would be so easy to get a career going over here in the coffee business if he didn't have something that looked good in his resume, like winning latte art competitions."

Lauren stared at Amy's ashamed expression. She couldn't imagine what the other woman was going through right now.

"He was good," Amy told them. "I asked him why he hadn't entered any championships here, and he told me he was afraid of losing." She chuckled without mirth. "How ironic! He was the best barista I've ever seen, and I've worked with plenty over the years, including some who *have* won major competitions. He didn't have anything to worry about."

"What did you do?" Lauren asked curiously.

"What could I do?" Amy sadly shook her head. "By that time, we'd advertised the evening latte art class, and he – we – thought it would damage our café's reputation if we suddenly printed a correction saying Gio actually wasn't a barista champion. I felt so stupid." Amy buried her face in her hands. "I thought it was all my fault – I trusted what he told me when we first met, working at the other café, and didn't do a background check on him when we went into business together." She wiped tears from her eyes. "I didn't think there was any need to."

"But you got involved romantically with him." Lauren narrowed her gaze.

"That was before I knew the truth," Amy replied. "He could be very charming, and eventually I fell for him.

But when he confessed everything, I was floored. I didn't know what to do. He said he couldn't afford to buy me out of the café right now, and that his feelings for me were real. He said I shouldn't let one mistake ruin our relationship."

"Could you have afforded to buy him out?" Zoe asked, her brown inquisitive.

"No." Amy shook her head. "I'm still paying off the business loan I got to open this place. Gio and I put in half each. If I'd gone to the bank, they might have lent me more money, but I was scared to overload myself with debt."

"That sounds wise," Lauren said. She was lucky that her grandmother had left her the café and cottage in her will. Otherwise, she didn't know if she could afford to run her own business.

"So Gio and I talked it over, and we decided to keep everything going for the moment. The business and – us. And then he was – you know."

"Who inherits Gio's share of the business?" Zoe asked.

"I do," Amy replied.

Lauren and Zoe stared at her.

"And he would have inherited my share if I'd died," Amy added hastily. "We had our wills drawn up by a lawyer – everything's above board."

"Apart from Giovanni's background," Zoe said.

CHAPTER 15

Lauren and Zoe discussed Amy's revelation on the drive home, detouring to a store that sold string art supplies, and a pet store.

"I can't even get excited right now about my new project," Zoe grumbled as she stared out of the window, looking at the passing trees. "I can't believe what Amy told us."

"I know." Lauren nodded as she kept her hands steady on the steering wheel.

"Hey!" Zoe tapped her cheek. "That gives Amy a motive. Now Giovanni's dead, she'll own the whole café."

"Do you really think she'd kill him, though?"

"Who knows?" Zoe shrugged. "I thought Amy was a sweet person who was a great teacher, and now I find out that she had a big secret."

"Mm." Lauren wasn't sure how to feel about Amy's confession. She could certainly sympathize with her – what would Lauren do if Zoe admitted she wasn't who she said she was? Except she'd known Zoe all her life, and her cousin didn't have a financial stake in the cat café. Not like Giovanni had in his Sacramento coffee shop with Amy.

"Do you think we should tell the police?" Zoe asked.

"About Amy inheriting Giovanni's share?"

"Yes!"

"No. I'm sure the Sacramento police will have checked who benefits. They might have already spoken to Amy about that aspect of the case."

"And she mightn't have told us." Zoe shook her head in wonder.

"Not everyone has to tell us everything."

"I just like knowing things, that's all." Zoe sighed.

"Mm-hm." Lauren certainly *knew* that.

When they arrived home, Zoe spread out her purchases on the kitchen table. "I'm going to get started with my string art – maybe it will help take my mind off everything."

"Good idea," Lauren said. She pulled out a small toy from her purse. "Annie, we're home."

"Brrt?" Annie wandered into the kitchen. She looked a little sleepy – maybe they'd interrupted her nap.

"I bought something for you." Lauren dangled the toy hedgehog in front of the cat. She squished the creature's stomach. "It has catnip in it."

"Brrt!" Annie's eyes rounded as she stared at the furry brown toy in Lauren's hand.

"That hedgehog is so cute." Zoe spoke. "So soft and cuddly. It makes me want to have one and I'm not a cat!"

"Here." Lauren placed the toy on the ground. Annie sniffed at it, then picked it up in her mouth and trotted off to the living room.

"I'm glad she likes it." Zoe grinned.

"Me, too."

Lauren watched her cousin tip out a pack of shiny silver nails onto the table.

"Do we have a hammer?" Zoe frowned. "I didn't think of that when I was at the store."

"There should be one somewhere." Lauren searched the utility drawer, which held tools that might come in handy one day – she didn't like to think of it as a 'junk' drawer.

"Here." She gave Zoe an old, heavy hammer.

"Thanks."

Bang! Bang! Bang!

Zoe hammered the nails into an owl pattern on a square of black canvas.

"I think I'll go to the living room." Lauren closed the kitchen door behind her, hoping Zoe would finish that part of her project soon. She hadn't realized string art was so noisy.

"Brrp?" Annie looked up from the sofa – she was stretched out over two seat cushions, the soft toy nestled close to her chest.

"Zoe's being creative," Lauren told her.

Annie closed her eyes as a faint *Bang!* sounded.

Lauren felt like doing the same.

***

The next morning, they opened the café right on time. Zoe had talked about her string art project last night. It had taken her a while to hammer in all the nails as specified in the pattern.

"Tonight I'm going to start making the picture with the pink, purple, and silver threads," she told Lauren as she sat behind the counter, waiting for their first customer. "This owl is going to look gorgeous!"

"It sounds interesting." Lauren shared a glance with Annie, who was cuddling her new toy in her cat bed. Annie put her paw over her ear, as if saying she didn't want to hear anything more about string art right now.

"It is! This could really be the one hobby for me."

"Are you sure?" Lauren teased.

"I could make tons of different designs," Zoe enthused. "I could make some for the cottage and ooh, this café of course, and then I could make a picture for Mrs. Finch, and Hans, and Ed, and—"

"And here's our first customer," Lauren told her.

Ms. Tobin entered the café wearing a pale blue skirt and a cream blouse. She waved to Lauren and Zoe, her expression bright.

Annie jumped down from her cat bed and trotted over to her. She'd left the toy hedgehog behind.

"Thank you, Annie, dear." Ms. Tobin smiled down at the cat.

"Brrt!" Annie led the way to a table in the middle of the room.

Lauren hurried over to take her order.

"I would love a large latte, Lauren," Ms. Tobin said, placing her tablet on the table. "And one of Ed's pastries, if they're ready."

"Of course." Lauren scratched out the order with her pencil and notepad. "They're cherry pinwheels today."

"Wonderful." Ms. Tobin pressed a button on her device and the screen lit up.

Lauren hurried back to the counter, pondering once again Ms. Tobin's new friendliness and more attractive clothes. She'd previously been their most difficult customer.

"She's glued to her screen again," Zoe whispered over the growling of the espresso machine. "I'm sure she's got a secret boyfriend."

"As long as whatever she's doing on that tablet keeps making her happy,"

Lauren said, steaming the milk. The hissing of the wand was a soothing backdrop to their conversation. "It's like she's a different woman."

"Maybe Frank needs to be doing whatever Ms. Tobin is," Zoe mused as she plated the pastry, glistening purple cherries atop golden flaky pastry. "He got so upset yesterday when Amy wouldn't give him a job. He could have killed Giovanni. What if he asked Gio to train him as a barista on the last night of latte art class? When we were eating cake? And Giovanni said no, so—" Zoe snapped her fingers "—Frank grabbed the knife later and stabbed him."

"Yesterday you thought it was Amy because she benefits from Giovanni's death," Lauren reminded her, as she pointed the nose of the milk jug towards the rich brown crema of the espresso, a peacock coming to life on the surface of the latte.

"Well, it could have been."

"Do you have anyone else in mind?" Lauren placed the coffee and the pastry on a tray.

"Judy and Casey."

"Really?"

"I don't think it was Casey," Zoe said in all seriousness. "Remember how worried she was when she thought her mom was going to be arrested?"

"And nobody seems to have heard anything more about that," Lauren replied.

"We should call Judy later today. See how she is. Grill her. Find out if they did arrest her."

"I'll take this over to Ms. Tobin." Lauren hurried over to her customer. She didn't want the latte to get cold while she and her cousin discussed the case.

"Oh," Ms. Tobin sighed softly as she stared at the tablet. Her smile made her appear a lot younger. She didn't seem to have heard Lauren's approach.

"Here you are, Ms. Tobin." Lauren gently placed the tray on the table.

"Thank you, dear." Ms. Tobin briefly looked up from the screen. Then her gaze dropped back down, as if she couldn't bear to look away from whatever had caught her attention. "I'm sure it will be delicious."

Lauren's eyebrows rose as she walked back to the counter. Something on that tablet was definitely making Ms. Tobin happy.

"I thought I'd call Judy this afternoon," Zoe announced.

"Okay," Lauren replied. She was curious whether Judy had been arrested. She hoped not.

"Ooh, I bet Mitch knows if Judy was detained." Zoe grinned. "You should call him and ask. You can even use my phone." She held out her device.

"I'm not doing that." Lauren shook her head.

"Why not – oh, hi, Hans."

Annie scampered over to the dapper gentleman.

"Hello, Lauren and Zoe." He bent a little stiffly. "And Annie, of course. What do you have there, *Liebchen*?"

Lauren noticed something furry and brown dangling from the cat's mouth.

"Brrp," Annie's voice was muffled.

"It's her new toy," Lauren told him. "I bought it for her yesterday."

"What a lucky girl you are." Hans beamed at Annie.

"Brrp." She slowly led him to a small table near the counter, then jumped up on the vacant seat, dropping the hedgehog on the table. She pushed the toy over to Hans with her paw.

"Oh, he is very nice." Hans studied the creature in all seriousness.

"He's got catnip inside." Lauren came over to take his order since he was occupied with Annie.

"Thank you for showing me, Annie." Hans nodded at the cat.

"Brrt." Annie reached out with her paw and hooked the toy toward her so it was directly in front of her on the table.

"What can I get you, Hans?" Lauren asked.

He glanced around the room. "I see I am your second customer today."

"I don't know what Ms. Tobin is doing on her tablet but she seems very engrossed in it." Lauren kept her voice low. She felt a little guilty talking about one of her customers to another.

"Ach. The gossip is she has an online boyfriend." Hans' faded blue eyes twinkled.

"Really?" Zoe had been right.

"It is big news at the senior center."

"Ms. Tobin goes there?"

"No." He shook his head. "But a friend of hers does, and says she does not have time to go out anymore because she is always emailing her boyfriend."

"Has she met him in real life?" Lauren asked curiously. Zoe's short period of internet dating hadn't turned out well.

"I do not think so. But why not ask her yourself?" His tone was gentle.

"She might not like that." Lauren was still getting used to the new, happier Ms. Tobin, and didn't want to do anything that would make the old, prickly version reappear.

"But it would make her feel good to know you took an interest."

"You think so?" Lauren furrowed her brow.

"*Ja.* She is always telling her friend about your café and how much she likes it – and Annie."

"She does?" Lauren was scared she would get permanent wrinkles at this rate as her frown deepened. "I would never have guessed."

"Some people have trouble expressing their feelings." Hans shrugged. "Her bark is worse than her bite – that is the correct expression?"

"Yes." Lauren nodded.

After taking his order for a mocha and a cherry pinwheel, she left Hans and Annie to enjoy their time together.

"What were you talking about?" Zoe whispered as she scanned Lauren's notepad. "I'll make the mocha so I can practice my peacock."

"You might have been right about Ms. Tobin." Lauren quickly filled her in on her conversation with Hans.

"I'm going to ask her." Zoe's eyes sparkled. "What's the worst she can do? Besides, she seems to be in a good mood today."

Zoe loaded up the tray and took it over to Hans. After talking to him and Annie for a moment, she made a beeline for Ms. Tobin's table. Lauren followed her. She didn't think it was a good idea to leave the two of them alone.

"Hi, Ms. Tobin," Zoe said brightly.

The older woman blinked at the intrusion, slowly looking up from her tablet.

"Hello, Zoe."

Zoe looked around the room, then bent down. "Is it true you've got a boyfriend on there?" She pointed to the tablet.

Lauren felt like clapping her hand over her eyes.

"Zoe!" she hissed. "I'm sorry, Ms. Tobin," she said in a louder voice. "We shouldn't have disturbed you."

"It's all right, dear." Ms. Tobin tapped her device. "It's true. I do have a gentleman friend. His name is Kenneth and he's working offshore at the moment."

"How did you meet him?" Zoe asked curiously.

"I was playing an online word game," Ms. Tobin replied. "And then a message from him popped up saying hello." She blushed. "It developed from there."

"What does Kenneth do?" Now it was Lauren's turn to be inquisitive.

"He's in the oil business," the older woman replied. "That's why we haven't met yet. But he's promised as soon as his contract is up he'll come and visit me. He's even planning a trip we can go on – he wants to go on a Caribbean cruise, but I think I'd prefer a Hawaiian one."

"Do you have a photo of him?" Zoe asked.

"Of course. Here." Ms. Tobin tapped a couple of buttons and an image of a handsome middle-aged man appeared on the screen. "Isn't he good looking?"

"He certainly is," Lauren agreed.

The image of a man in his fifties, with windswept brown hair, and wearing jeans and a casual shirt, greeted her gaze.

"Unfortunately, he's having some financial problems at the moment." Ms. Tobin sighed. "The bank over there won't accept his paychecks, so he has to wait until he gets back to the States, and then deposit all his salary."

"His employer isn't depositing his earnings into his U.S. bank account?" Zoe frowned. "Can't he use his ATM card from his American bank account to access a machine over there to withdraw his earnings?"

"I just said his employer can't pay him while he's over there." Ms. Tobin's voice sounded a little frosty. "The banks over there won't accept those deposits."

"It sounds a little strange." Lauren kept her voice low.

Zoe stared at the middle-aged man's image on the screen, and tapped her cheek. "You aren't sending him any money, are you?"

"Whatever do you mean?" Ms. Tobin flushed, her gaze dropping to the screen.

"It could be a scam," Zoe continued.

"A scam?" Ms. Tobin's eyes widened.

"It's super fishy that his employer can't pay him while he's over there." Zoe nodded to herself. "And now he's asking you for money."

"How did you know?"

"I read up on internet scams a while ago, when I joined some dating sites," Zoe admitted. "I wanted to make sure I wouldn't get duped."

"But he said ..." Ms. Tobin's voice trembled. "He said ..." She shook her head and stood. "No. I don't believe you. You just don't want me to be happy." She glared at them. "So what if he needs a little money from me? I can afford it. In a few months' time, his contract will be up and he'll be able to visit me. We might even get married. And you *won't* be invited to the wedding!"

Ms. Tobin stormed out of the café, slamming the entrance door behind her.

"Wow." Zoe's eyes rounded.

"I hope he's not a scammer," Lauren murmured.

Annie looked up from her conversation with Hans, her ears pricked and twitching at the crashing sound of the door.

"I do," Zoe replied. "It would be worse for her if he was a deadbeat boyfriend – then she'd never get rid of him because he'd know she has money. But if he is a scammer, maybe her friends can talk some sense into her, or we can find some proof to show her."

"I thought you wanted to investigate Giovanni's death." Lauren raised her eyebrow.

"And you didn't think it was a good idea." Zoe pouted. "We haven't done much at all. So—" she dug out her phone from her pocket. "I'm going to call Judy right now instead of waiting for this afternoon, and invite her to come over for a coffee on the house. And then I'm going to grill her!"

"Do you think that's a good idea?"

"Yes," Zoe insisted. "She asked us to investigate at our little class reunion at Casey's café, remember?"

"I certainly do."

"So I think it's time we picked up the pace. Actually do something!"

"We discovered that Casey was stealing coffee beans," Lauren pointed out as the two of them headed back to the counter.

"That wasn't much." Zoe waved her hand dismissively. "But we did find out that Frank has a temper when he doesn't get something he wants."

"True," Lauren said thoughtfully. "And we found out that Giovanni was a fraud."

"I wonder if the police know about that? Maybe you could discuss that with Mitch."

"Maybe."

Before Lauren could think up a reason *not* to do that, the entrance door opened.

Mitch stood in the doorway, scanning the room for a second, before striding to the counter – and Lauren. It had been three days since their last date – not that she was counting.

"Hi." Was the memory of their kiss reflected in his eyes?

"Hi." Lauren smiled.

"Ask him." Zoe whispered in her cousin's ear, and nudged her in the ribs as well. "And about the *other thing* as well." She stepped away from Lauren. "Hi, Mitch." Zoe acted as if she hadn't hissed something to Lauren. "I think Ed needs some help, and I'm going to call Judy." She giggled as she pushed open the swinging door into the kitchen.

"What did Zoe say to you?" Mitch asked curiously.

What *had* her cousin murmured to her? Lauren's brain paused for a second.

"Oh." She started as she guessed what the second thing was. "Zoe's wondering if you know anyone who might be interested in a blind date with her."

His eyes crinkled at the corners. "I'll give it some thought. Anything else?"

She hesitated.

"Did you know Giovanni wasn't really a barista champion?"

He frowned. "I haven't heard that specifically, but I'm not on the case. I spoke to a friend yesterday about the murder, but he didn't have any new information – or any that he could share with me. How did you find that out about Giovanni?"

Lauren quickly filled him in on Amy's revelation yesterday. "And they made out wills in each other's favor," she finished.

"That's not uncommon with business partners," he told her. "The Sacramento detectives would have checked into that aspect of the case."

There was a silence. Lauren could hear Hans' quiet voice talking to Annie. She desperately tried to think of something to say. But now all she could think of was that amazing kiss they'd shared on Saturday night.

Was Mitch thinking about it too? Or was he wondering what sort of cupcake to buy, or about the investigation into Giovanni's murder?

"I'd love a latte," he spoke.

"Sure." Heat hit her cheeks. He'd been thinking about coffee. That was all.

"And—" he cleared his throat. "Are you busy on the weekend? I thought you could show me your favorite hiking trail."

"I'd love to," she replied quickly.

"Great. How about Sunday? Ten o'clock?"

"Yes." She busied herself making his coffee. Would she *ever* not be totally aware of his presence?

"I'll pick you up."

"Okay." She hoped she could manage more than one-word sentences on their hike. While not being a hot and sweaty mess. It *was* summer. "That would be great."

They smiled at each other, until Zoe came out of the kitchen's swinging doors.

"Judy's coming over this afternoon." She grinned.

***

"I hope it won't be too busy while Judy's here," Lauren fretted an hour later. Business had picked up and the early lunch crowd had arrived. As well as cupcakes and Ed's pastries, they also served freshly filled paninis, the bread supplied by a regional bakery.

"I'll talk to her while you serve customers," Zoe teased. "It will be fine, you'll see."

"I hope so," Lauren replied doubtfully.

But Zoe turned out to be right. By the time Judy arrived just after three o'clock, the crowd of customers had thinned. Lauren might even get to be in on the conversation.

"You aren't going to interrogate her, are you?" Lauren murmured as Judy stood at the *Please Wait to be Seated sign*.

"I'll be good," Zoe promised, hurrying to greet the older woman.

"Brrt!" Annie padded over to Judy.

"You are even prettier than last time, Annie." Judy beamed down at the cat. "I wish I could have a cat like you."

"I'm glad you were able to make it," Zoe told her. "Annie will find us a table where we can all catch up."

Only three tables were occupied, and everyone had received their orders.

"Brrp." Annie led the way to a secluded table at the back of the room –

big enough for four. Her plumy silver-gray tail waved in the air as Zoe and Judy followed her.

"Would you like something to drink, Judy?" Lauren arrived at the table Annie had chosen. The feline was already sitting on a chair, her gaze divided between all three females. The toy hedgehog hadn't accompanied her, however.

"I would love a mocha," Judy admitted. "If you have time to make one."

"We should all have one," Zoe declared.

"We'll be back in a minute." Lauren smiled at Judy.

Zoe accompanied her cousin back to the espresso machine.

"It will be faster if we make them together," Lauren said. "You do the milk and I'll make the espressos."

"Roger, boss." Zoe grinned.

The crunching grind of the coffee beans and the hissing of the milk wand soothed Lauren's nerves. What were they going to say to Judy? Or perhaps she shouldn't worry about it – Zoe had probably already planned what she was going to say.

They returned to Annie and Judy. The feline seemed to be lapping up Judy's soft sweet talk.

"Here we are," Zoe said cheerfully, putting a mug down in front of Judy.

"It looks wonderful." Judy admired the design of the slightly wobbly peacock.

Once they all sat down, Zoe launched with, "Did the police arrest you?"

"Zoe!" Lauren wondered if she really should be shocked at the question.

"No." Judy stirred her coffee, then looked at them. "I know why you're asking. Casey told me she visited to ask for advice because she overhead the detectives talk about getting a warrant. I want to thank you for listening to her and not brushing her off. But there's nothing to worry about."

She hesitated and looked around, as if to make sure nobody would eavesdrop. The table Annie had chosen was far enough away from the other customers for that not to be a possibility.

"What is it?" Zoe urged.

"I'm very embarrassed about this." Judy sighed, her gaze dropping to her beverage. "But I had a DUI. Many years ago," she added hastily. "So that's why—"

"Your fingerprints are in the system," Zoe finished. "Casey told us about that."

"So when the detectives checked the knife for prints, they must have found mine on there because I helped Amy clean up after we ate the cake at the end of class," Judy added.

"And that's why they were talking about getting an arrest warrant," Lauren added.

"They mustn't have had enough evidence, though," Judy said. "Because I haven't received another visit from them."

"The killer mustn't have wiped off the knife properly," Zoe declared. "Or, maybe he did!"

"Brrt?" Annie's eyes widened as she stared at Zoe.

"What if the murderer was at class – he or she is one of us – and they saw you handle the cake knife. And then, after they stabbed Giovanni, they carefully wiped their fingerprints but left yours to implicate you – or maybe they even used gloves, so they wouldn't even have to wipe the knife, so your fingerprints would remain on the handle."

"That is genius thinking," Lauren said with admiration.

"Thanks." Zoe winked at her.

"But who on earth would do that?" Judy asked. "And why would they want to frame me?"

"So the police don't think it was them," Zoe replied. "They get away with it, and you go to jail – or maybe not, since they haven't arrested you yet."

"I knew I was right asking you two to investigate." Judy sipped her mocha. "Mm. This is delicious, girls. So, what else have you found out?"

Lauren and Zoe exchanged a glance. It wouldn't be fair to tell Judy that her daughter had stolen coffee beans from her employer – not when it looked like Casey had come clean and had left that coffee shop for Amy's. Lauren doubted that Casey would steal from Amy – the teen seemed to admire the café owner.

"Frank has a temper," Zoe admitted.

"He wants to get some barista training," Lauren added.

"And Amy – well, maybe Amy should tell you that," Zoe prevaricated.

Lauren guessed Zoe meant about Amy benefitting from Giovanni's death.

"Ooh!" Zoe drew in a breath. "Giovanni—" she stopped with a strangled squeak and looked apologetically at Lauren. "We promised not to say anything," she told Judy in a quieter voice. "Sorry."

"I'm sure it's okay to tell me," Judy cajoled. "Casey is going to be working for Amy so if there's anything I need to know about the café, I think you should let me know."

"It doesn't affect Casey's employment there," Lauren said. Unless word got out somehow about Giovanni not really being a barista champion. Then Amy and her café might be tainted by association, business would drop off, and Casey might lose her job because of lack of customers. But Lauren didn't want to think about that happening.

"Have you found out anything else?" Judy asked curiously.

"Nope." Zoe shook her head.

Annie finding the fondant flower flitted through Lauren's mind, but she decided not to tell Judy about that. If it was from the cake they enjoyed at the last latte art class, that meant that either Frank, Judy, or Casey had dropped it here in the café. Unless she or Zoe had somehow transferred it from class to this very room.

She glanced over at Zoe, wondering if her cousin had just had the same thought. Zoe met her gaze and inclined her head so slightly, Lauren wondered if she'd imagined the movement.

"I just hope they catch the killer soon." Judy finished her coffee and looked at her watch. "I'd better go. Casey is meeting with Amy this evening to go over her new part-time position, and I'm going with her, to say hello to Amy. I think this new job will suit Casey much better." She hesitated. "I didn't like to tell my daughter, but I thought the coffee where she used to work was *bitter*."

CHAPTER 16

"I hope Judy's not upset I questioned her," Zoe said two days later. They hadn't heard from Judy, Casey, Frank, or Amy since then.

"She didn't seem to be," Lauren replied, counting how many triple chocolate cupcakes were left in the glass case. Three. And five raspberry swirls.

Ed's pastries had sold out and it was just after two o'clock. Mrs. Finch had been in, as well as Claire and her little girl Molly.

Ms. Tobin had not come in since she'd stormed off in a huff over her online boyfriend drama. Lauren hoped she would be okay.

"We should have plenty of time to get to the vet's this evening," Zoe said. "The appointment's six-thirty."

"We should make it for sure," Lauren agreed. It was time for Annie's yearly checkup, and Lauren favored a specialist cat vet in Sacramento.

The rest of the afternoon passed quickly, and Zoe stacked up the chairs on the tables in record time as Lauren vacuumed the floor.

"All set for the vet, Annie?" Lauren asked.

Annie sat up in her pink cat bed in the café and stared at Lauren with big green eyes.

"Brrp." Her mouth tilted down at the corners.

"It's just a little checkup. Nothing to worry about," Lauren told her. "Zoe and I will be with you."

"Brrt." Annie seemed a little cheered.

"And you like Dr Tegan," Lauren encouraged her. "She knows all about cats, doesn't she?"

A mumbled "Brrt."

"Never mind," Zoe told her. "We'll come home as soon as your checkup is complete. We can watch something good on TV tonight, and you can help Lauren with her knitting."

"Brrt!" Annie perked up.

Lauren wasn't sure whether it was mentioning TV, or knitting. Sometimes she didn't think she'd ever finish her scarf, but she'd certainly get the needles out tonight, and dangle the wool in front of Annie to play with.

They popped Annie into a green cat carrier and placed her in the car, securing her with the seatbelt.

Lauren and Zoe chatted about their weekend plans, Zoe teasing her cousin about her upcoming hike with Mitch.

"Annie and I will make our own plans, won't we, Annie?" Zoe twisted around in her seat to include the cat in the conversation. "We could visit Mrs. Finch."

"Brrp," Annie agreed, staring out of the window at the passing scenery of small fruit orchards.

The checkup went smoothly, Dr Tegan greeting them with a smile.

"Annie looks great," she praised. "Keep doing whatever it is you're doing with her."

"That wasn't so bad, was it?" Lauren asked Annie as they returned to the car, Annie still in her carrier.

"Brrt!" Annie murmured, her expression more cheerful now the visit was over.

Lauren started the engine when a *ping* sounded. Zoe stared at her phone.

"What is it?" Lauren asked.

"It's a text from Judy. She wants us to all meet up at Amy's café."

"When?"

"Now."

"That's short notice, isn't it?" Lauren frowned. "We've got Annie with us. I'm not going to leave her in the car while we're in the coffee shop."

Zoe tapped away at her phone. A few seconds later, another *ping*.

"Judy says Annie can join us. Amy's cool with it."

"She is?" Lauren frowned. Her cat café had been certified as one – but she didn't know what the laws were in Sacramento concerning cats in regular cafes.

"Amy's closed the café for the day, so we'll be there after hours," Zoe relayed, checking her device.

"What do you think, Annie?" Lauren turned to the cat in the backseat. "Would you like to go to Amy's coffee shop first, or would you like to go straight home?"

"Brrt," Annie replied, looking at Lauren.

"I think that means she wants to visit Amy's," Zoe put in.

"Yes." Lauren pulled out into the traffic. She knew roughly where the café was from the vet's. "But I don't want to stay long."

"Agreed," Zoe replied. "I wouldn't mind another one of Amy's coffees, though."

"True." Lauren felt she could do with a little pick-me-up. "We'll ask if Annie can have a bowl of water."

"Brrp," Annie seemed to agree.

A short while later, they pulled up outside Amy's café. There was only one other car there – Judy's beige station wagon.

"Where is everyone?" Zoe frowned.

"Maybe we're the first ones here, apart from Judy," Lauren said.

"Amy probably parks around the back," Zoe suggested.

Lauren unbuckled Annie's seatbelt. "We won't stay long," she told her, gently picking up the carrier.

Annie's ears pricked as she was transported toward the café, sporting a maple and white exterior.

"Hello?" Lauren called out when they reached the entrance. She peered in through the large plate glass window but couldn't see anyone inside.

"We're here," Zoe said in a loud voice, pushing open the door.

"Hello, girls," Judy suddenly appeared in front of them, wearing pale blue slacks with big patchwork pockets and a matching short sleeved t-shirt. "Annie, you're just so cute again."

"Brrp." Annie sounded a little subdued.

"She's just had a checkup at the vet's," Lauren told the older woman.

"Is there anything wrong?" Judy asked curiously.

"No." Lauren shook her head. "Everything's fine. It was just routine."

"That's good to hear." Judy smiled as she led them to the café area.

"Where's Amy?" Zoe asked, scanning the space. All the tables were vacant.

"She's in the office, finishing up her paperwork," Judy replied. "Frank should be here any minute. I asked Casey if she wanted to come but she said she had homework to do." She lowered her voice. "She might be a bit embarrassed about asking you for help when she thought I was going to be arrested."

"That's understandable," Lauren replied, wondering if Casey's nonattendance had anything to do with the fact that she and Zoe knew about the stolen coffee beans.

"Well, sit down you two – three," Judy amended as she glanced at Annie. "Amy said I could get the espressos started."

"She did?" Lauren exchanged a glance with Zoe as they chose a table near the counter.

"She showed me how to do it just before you arrived," Judy confided.

"Could I get a bowl of water for Annie?" Lauren requested.

"Of course." Judy bustled behind the counter, placing a white bowl of water on the table.

"Is it okay to let Annie out of the carrier?" Zoe asked.

"Certainly," Judy said. "Amy said it was fine."

"Okay." Lauren glanced around, checking the entrance door was closed. So was the door that led to the office down the hallway. She trusted Annie not to run off, but if something unexpected startled her, her feline instincts might take over, urging her to escape through the nearest open door.

"Brrp." Once Annie was out of confinement, she lapped at the water, her little pink tongue darting in and out.

"She is so adorable." Judy sighed. "Don't worry, I'll make sure she goes to a loving family. I'd take her myself, but my husband is allergic to cats and I don't want to divorce him."

"What are you talking about?" Lauren's senses went on alert at the older woman's words.

"I don't want to do this, but you've left me no choice," Judy told them. "I hate to be so dramatic, but you won't be getting out of here alive!"

"What?" Zoe squeaked.

Judy tsked. "Haven't you girls worked it out yet?" She placed her hands on her hips.

Lauren's eyes widened. "You're the killer? But why?"

"I was leaning toward Frank." Zoe sounded disappointed.

"A double bluff," Lauren said slowly.

"Very good," Judy praised. "It's just a shame – for you – and Zoe – you didn't come to that conclusion sooner. I thought you would, considering all the poking around you've been doing. I couldn't risk you realizing I was the killer."

"But you wanted us to investigate Giovanni's murder," Zoe protested.

"Because I didn't think you would get anywhere." Judy laughed harshly. "I was wrong."

Annie's ears flattened at the sound.

"When I visited you two days ago, you surprised me with everything you found out, as well as those secrets you wouldn't divulge. What were they, Zoe?" Judy sounded very interested.

Zoe mimed zipping her lips.

"It doesn't really matter," Judy told her. "Once I get rid of you two, I'll be in the clear. The police will never guess it was me."

"Where's Amy?" Lauren frantically looked around, as if expecting Amy to magically pop up out of nowhere.

"She's not here." Judy smiled, but her green eyes remained hard. "She decided to close early today. Casey told me."

"How did you get in here?" Zoe asked.

"I swiped a key the other night when I visited with Casey," Judy replied. "It was easy. Amy had paperwork for Casey to fill out for her new job here and she left us alone for a moment. While my daughter was busy writing down her details, I stole a set of keys I saw poking out from under a stack of papers." She shook her head. "Amy isn't very neat, you know."

"So Amy's not coming. Nor Frank." Lauren felt horribly alone – apart from Annie and Zoe.

"That's right. And nobody knows you're here." Judy smiled chillingly.

Lauren squared her shoulders. "You still haven't told us why you killed Giovanni."

"Because he was a jerk." Judy suddenly glared at them, her face a mask of disgust. "He wanted to take Casey away from me."

"But why?" Zoe asked, her eyes wide.

"Because," Judy drew in a huge breath, "he was her father."

"No way!" Zoe stared at her.

"You won't believe the shock I received when I saw him at the first latte art class. I didn't think he'd recognized me, and I pretended I didn't know him at all, but afterward, when I was going to the ladies' room, he accosted me. He'd recognized me after all."

"What did you do?" Lauren asked.

"I tried to be cool and calm, but I think he saw through my façade." Judy's lips tightened. "He asked me about Casey and I showed him my wedding ring and told him I was married, and my husband was Casey's father."

"But he didn't believe you?" Zoe guessed.

"That's right. I didn't want to go back to the second latte art class, but Casey insisted. And I didn't want her to get suspicious about why I didn't want to go back – you know what teenagers are like. They can imagine all sorts of things."

"And then what happened?" Lauren asked, enthralled despite herself. Annie sat next to her, her ears pricked at full attention.

"Giovanni took me aside after class and told me he knew he was Casey's dad. He said Casey looked just like his mother did around the same age. And that Casey was a talented barista, just like him. He wouldn't believe me when I lied and told him he wasn't her father."

"How did you two meet?" Lauren asked.

"I spent a summer in Italy after college. I fell in love with Giovanni – although that wasn't his name back then. His real name was Roberto Zampullo and I thought he felt the same about me. But when I told him I was pregnant, he couldn't get away from me fast enough. He denied it was his. Do you know how hurtful that was? He had been the only one at the time – in fact, he'd only been my second lover."

"What did you do?" Zoe asked.

"I flew back home to Seattle. I wanted to keep the baby, but I didn't know if I could do it on my own. I was scared to tell my parents, afraid they would kick me out. And then I met my husband. I think we both knew right away that we could be happy together. We had a whirlwind romance and got married six weeks later."

"And you didn't tell him about the baby?" Lauren guessed.

"Not until we'd had sex," Judy replied. "And then I told him it was his."

"And he believed you?"

"Why wouldn't he?" Judy frowned. "His positive attitude toward the baby made me realize I'd wasted myself on Giovanni. I was determined that man would never ruin my life again."

"Until—" Zoe prompted.

"Until he turned up as the teacher at latte art class. How dare he! After the second class – and you have no idea how difficult it was to be right there next to him, having him tell me what I was doing wrong with my designs – he told me he wanted to get to know Casey as her father and train her for barista competitions. He didn't care that I was happy with her stepfather, who's been a wonderful dad to her. All he cared about was himself, exactly the same as when I told him I was pregnant."

"But how did you find time to kill him?" Lauren asked. "We were all there."

"Not all of you." Judy tossed off a laugh. "You and Zoe had left. I was helping Amy in the kitchen clean up the dishes after everyone finished eating the cake, and that's when I got the idea to kill Giovanni, when I was handling the knife. Then Giovanni came into the kitchen and told us to leave the dishes until tomorrow." Her mouth tightened. "I don't know how Amy stood being bossed around like that.

"Frank said he wanted to buy the coffee beans and Giovanni told Amy to take Frank and Casey to the office since he closed down the register, and he would join them in a minute after he made a quick phone call."

"Then what happened?" Zoe stared at Judy.

"Giovanni started telling me how he wanted to get to know Casey, blah blah

blah. His phone call excuse was a ruse. By this time I'd had enough. He told me to follow him to the office and buy some beans, and tomorrow he was going to tell Casey that he was her father. I couldn't allow that to happen! While his back was turned, I grabbed the cake knife. He didn't even look behind him once to see if I was following him, he just assumed I would.

"When he stopped at the store cupboard, to get out the beans, I realized this was my chance. That's when I stabbed him."

"But you didn't have blood on you," Lauren commented.

"I was lucky." Judy smiled. "I hadn't thought about that happening. I just wanted to get Giovanni out of my – and Casey's – life."

"I didn't see any blood on the napkin and the fondant flower." Zoe crinkled her brow.

"I got lucky again. I didn't have any blood on my fingers after I killed him. But I did have some frosting on my hand. That's why I wiped it with a paper napkin I had in my purse. I must have picked up the napkin when we were eating the cake, and put it in my purse absentmindedly."

"So you dropped the pink fondant flower in our café," Lauren surmised.

"I must have." Judy shrugged. "I stuck the napkin into my handbag after I killed him. Then I forgot about it because it sank to the bottom of my bag – you know how that happens."

"Oh, yeah." Zoe nodded.

"If the detective had searched my purse, I would have told him that dirty napkin was from eating the cake – and I was trying to be discreet about having messy fingers. But somehow when I was at your café, the napkin must have dropped out of my bag. I know I had to rummage through it to find my phone while I was there."

"But weren't you questioned about where you were when Giovanni was stabbed?" Lauren probed.

"I told the police I was in the bathroom." Judy airily waved a hand in the air. "They couldn't disprove that. When Amy asked me about it later, I told her Giovanni was on the phone when I left the kitchen to go to the bathroom, and then I joined them in the office."

"Why did he move to the States?" Lauren asked curiously.

"He wanted a fresh start." Judy laughed mirthlessly. "Can you believe that? He knew I grew up in Seattle, so he probably thought he was safe living in California. But a couple of years ago my husband got a job promotion which meant we had to move here.

"He said he'd told Amy he changed his name to honor his dead best friend – he neglected to tell her he'd done some silly things in his youth and had a minor criminal record, as well as trying to hide from me – or any other girls he got pregnant, probably. Even if I'd tried to track him down in Italy, how could I if he was going under Giovanni now, and not Roberto?"

"Was he really a barista back then?" Lauren asked curiously.

"Oh, yes." Judy nodded. "That's how we met. I went into this little café in Florence where he worked with his best friend, the real Giovanni, and he made me the most wonderful cappuccino.

There was a spark between us from the start. And he asked me out right away. Of course I said yes. He was impossibly good looking – even better looking back then. And his accent!" She fanned herself, then sobered. "I let my hormones get the better of me."

"I'm sure if you tell the police everything, they'd be sympathetic," Zoe offered.

"No." Judy shook her head. "I'd still go to jail. Who would be there for Casey? She still has two years of school to get through, and I'm going to help her apply for colleges. It's all very well to want to be a barista and compete, but she's going to need a job that pays the bills when she's an adult. What happens if she hurts her wrist with all that latte art wiggling to get the perfect design on the coffee? She needs an education to fall back on."

"Your husband could look after her?" Lauren suggested.

"Dean would do all he can, but my baby needs her mother. I got rid of Giovanni – I'm not going to let that be in vain. Now it's your turn!"

Judy pulled out a long, sharp knife from the front pocket of her slacks. It glinted in the early evening sun streaming through the large glass windows.

Lauren and Zoe scrambled to their feet, their chairs clattering to the floor. Annie's fur and tail puffed out as she jumped from her chair to the top of the table.

"Your cat isn't going to save you," Judy scoffed. "No one is going to save you."

"That's what you think!" Zoe curled her hands into fists.

Lauren caught her cousin's gaze. Judy stood in front of them, the wickedly long knife in her hand. But the path to the entrance door was unblocked. If they could make a dash for it, and if Judy hadn't locked them in, there was a chance they would make it!

Annie knocked the water bowl over with her shoulder. The water splashed onto Judy, distracting her.

Lauren grabbed Annie and ran toward the door, Zoe close on her heels.

"Try these coffee beans!" Zoe snatched a bag of beans from the counter as she raced past and threw them at Judy's head.

"Ow!" Judy screamed as the twelve-ounce bag hit her temple.

A clatter filled the air as Lauren wrenched open the door and ran to the car. She hoped it was the knife falling to the ground.

"Let's go!" She placed Annie on the backseat and gunned the engine.

"Do it!" Zoe locked the car doors and clicked her seatbelt into place.

"Brrt!"

Lauren slammed her foot on the accelerator, holding her breath until they were a good distance away from the café.

"Phew!" Zoe fanned herself. "That was close."

"Brrt!"

***

Once they'd driven a couple of blocks, Lauren pulled over and called the police.

"I just hope they get there in time to catch Judy." Zoe shivered.

"Me, too." Lauren nodded. "But where would she go? Unless she has a ton of money in her purse, they'll be able to track her if she uses her credit card, or tries to catch a plane."

"I can't believe she killed Giovanni." Zoe shook her head. "She seemed like such a nice lady."

"I know."

"Brrt." Annie sounded sad.

EPILOGUE

The next day, Mitch came into the café. Lauren and Zoe had opened an hour later than usual. They'd had to give statements to the Sacramento police the previous evening, and as soon as they had arrived home, the three of them had gone straight to bed.

Now, Lauren looked at him apprehensively as he strode toward her.

"They caught her," he told her.

"Good." Lauren gripped the edge of the counter. She'd been exhausted last night, but had woken up a couple of times, wondering if Judy was somehow on her way to the cottage right now, with murderous intent. She was just thankful Annie hadn't woken – she didn't want her to have scary thoughts like that.

"She was at home, packing. Her daughter was at a friend's place and her husband was stuck at work."

"What did Judy say?" Lauren asked.

"She confessed." He shook his head. "It was as if she knew there wasn't any other option once the police arrived. Everything was done properly, but she waived her right to an attorney. She's going to plead guilty."

"I feel sorry for Casey, and Judy's husband."

"Yeah." His dark brown gaze caught hers. "I just wish you hadn't been involved."

"So do I." Lauren shuddered as she thought of last night's events.

Mitch gently placed his hand over hers.

"We didn't know she was the killer when we agreed to meet her at Amy's café yesterday," Lauren said, the warmth of his touch stirring her senses. "We thought everyone was going to be there."

"And when you found out they weren't?"

"She had a knife. Judy wasn't going to stand there and watch me call 911."

"I get it." He sighed. "I worry about you. I don't want to, but I do. I guess it's something I'll have to get used to."

Annie wandered over to the two of them. Zoe was in the kitchen, telling Ed all about last night. There were only a couple of customers, and they were occupied with eating cupcakes and drinking coffee.

"Brrt!" *Yes, it is.*

***

Later that day, Ms. Tobin entered the café. She scanned the room, her gaze lighting on a couple of tables that were occupied, as if not wanting an audience for what she was about to do, then walked over to the counter.

"Hi, Ms. Tobin," Lauren said politely. The older woman wore a fawn skirt and cream blouse, the same outfit she'd worn previously. It looked much better on her than the dull brown colors she'd favored until recently.

Was her most difficult customer going to berate her for telling her to be wary of her online boyfriend, who was most likely a scammer?

Annie watched from her cat bed, her expression alert and her ears pricked. But she seemed to sense that Ms. Tobin did not want to be led to a table just now.

"I want to apologize," she told Lauren and Zoe in a low voice.

"You do?" Zoe's eyes rounded.

"Yes." Ms. Tobin nodded. "You were right." She sighed. "After you told me Kenneth—" her voice hardened slightly on the man's name "—could be a scammer, I spent the rest of the day reading about romance scams and I found out—" her breath hitched "—that he's been contacting other women and telling them the same story. One of them posted his photo on a forum, and it was the same one he sent to me. He even told one lady that he would take her on a Hawaiian cruise! *I* suggested we do that."

"I'm sorry," Lauren replied.

"Me, too." Zoe gave her a wary smile.

"I was so stupid, blindly trusting someone I met online." She shook her head in disgust. "I can't believe I fell for it."

"You mustn't blame yourself," Lauren said impulsively.

"Yeah." Zoe nodded. "It could happen to anyone. I've had my share of online dating disasters, and I thought I was pretty savvy about the whole thing."

"Thank you, girls." Ms. Tobin managed a brief smile. "After the way I spoke to you, you're under no obligation to be nice to me." She looked around the room. "I do like coming here and saying hello to Annie. As well as enjoying your coffee and baking, Lauren. And Zoe, you're such a cheerful person."

"Thank you," Lauren replied softly.

"Brrt?" Annie padded over to Ms. Tobin.

"A table would be lovely, Annie." She looked uncertainly at Lauren and Zoe for a split-second. "If I'm still welcome here?"

"Of course." Lauren smiled at her.

"Yep." Zoe nodded.

"Brrt!" Annie led the way to a table in the middle of the room, and jumped up on the chair opposite Ms. Tobin.

Lauren watched the older woman talk to Annie, then begin to rise.

"Don't tell me she's coming over to the counter to order," Zoe murmured, her eyes widening. "That will be a first."

"Why don't we let her enjoy her chat with Annie? I think both of them would like that." Lauren whipped out her order pad and started toward Ms. Tobin's table.

"I'll come with you." Zoe grinned.

AUTHOR'S NOTE AND LIST OF TITLES

Annie is based on my own Norwegian Forest Cat, who was also called Annie.

I hope you enjoyed reading this mystery. Sign up to my newsletter at http://www.JintyJames.com and be among the first to discover when my next book is published!

Have you read:

Purrs and Peril – A Norwegian Forest Cat Café Cozy Mystery – Book 1

Meow Means Murder – A Norwegian Forest Cat Café Cozy Mystery – Book 2

<u>Maddie Goodwell Series (fun witch cozies)</u>

Spells and Spiced Latte - A Coffee Witch Cozy Mystery - Maddie Goodwell 1

Visions and Vanilla Cappuccino - A Coffee Witch Cozy Mystery - Maddie Goodwell 2

Magic and Mocha – A Coffee Witch Cozy Mystery – Maddie Goodwell 3

Enchantments and Espresso – A Coffee Witch Cozy Mystery – Maddie Goodwell 4

Familiars and French Roast - A Coffee Witch Cozy Mystery – Maddie Goodwell 5

Incantations and Iced Coffee – A Coffee Witch Cozy Mystery – Maddie Goodwell 6